ARC 486
K F #88

# Bird
# on the
# Wing

Books by Winifred Madison

*Maria Luisa*
*Max's Wonderful Delicatessen*
*Growing Up in a Hurry*
*Bird on the Wing*

# Bird
# on the
# Wing

## by
## Winifred
## Madison

Little, Brown and Company
Boston · Toronto

FIRST EDITION

T 03/74

Library of Congress Cataloging in Publication Data

Madison, Winifred.
  Bird on the wing.

  [1. Weaving--Fiction. 2. Runaways--Fiction]
I. Title.
PZ7.M2652Bi        [Fic]        73-17009
ISBN 0-316-54361-6

*Published simultaneously in Canada*
*by Little, Brown & Company (Canada) Limited*

PRINTED IN THE UNITED STATES OF AMERICA

1

For Deborah

# I
# Lincoln,
# Nebraska

It had been the longest and loneliest year of her life. And it wasn't over yet; three months to go. Elizabeth had lived in Lincoln since June, but she never really saw herself there. When she thought of herself, she was always back in Sacramento, swimming or riding in the red Porsche with Rick, and sometimes Ken and Linda too, tearing along the foothills. Was it possible that she had thrown her head back and laughed so much then when now she never laughed at all?

What memories she had were vivid, but polishing them too often had crystallized them, making them short and false, like TV commercials. Was California really so much the unreal TV world it now seemed?

"Never mind," she comforted herself. "Three months until June and then I'll be back, and it will be real once more." She saw herself all glowing and lovely, getting off the plane, while Rick, Linda and Ken waited to embrace her. California was waiting for her like a promise, the carrot in front of a donkey. She could see nothing else but that, and the thought of the Golden State succored her through a freezing winter.

Then one day in March, spring came unexpectedly. One soft day was followed by another and even a third. Walking home from school, Elizabeth was amazed that this city, so blistering the summer before and so bone-

2

chilling cold that winter, was capable of such a gentle spring. For the first time she looked around her.

"It's not really all that bad," she thought. In fact, the newer sections of Lincoln were not very different from certain parts of Sacramento.

A green fuzz promising leaves softened the trees. Dandelions with round, childlike faces peered out of lawns that would soon be greening. And above it all, a benevolent sun warmed the earth and shone on gossiping housewives and streets full of children — where had they come from all of a sudden? — already out with roller skates, balls and jumping ropes.

Yet Elizabeth was aware of more than the beauty of the day. In the block behind her, among other students ambling home, Daniel Wilson was striding along. Long legs and a purposeful walk, as though he at any rate were really going somewhere. She slowed her pace, hoping he would catch up to her. She wished she had brushed her hair before leaving school so the sun would make it shine like pale silk. And she regretted not leaving her coat at home, but no, Lorene had said better take it, it would probably turn cold, and didn't Elizabeth know about the freaky Lincoln weather and that this was a false spring. So all day long she carried the heavy thing on her arm.

"If he asks me this time, I'll go. Anywhere. To Shug's for a Coke or even a walk around the block," she said to herself. It was perhaps the first social thought she had had since coming to Lincoln. Last fall Daniel had asked her to the Drama Club play, to join the Media Club, to go with him to numerous concerts and dances, and now she could only sigh about the idiocy that had made

her say no. Well, she was sorry. She hadn't gone anywhere for almost a year.

"Hello, Elizabeth!"

Her heartbeat quickened ever so lightly as he caught
up with her and slackened his own pace to match hers.
The rough jacket he wore brushed against her arm, and
she would have liked it if he'd put his arm around her.
It was a long time since she'd been close to a boy.

"What do you think of our weather? Can California
compete with this?"

This was bait, and she laughed it off. One had to be
careful about being a California chauvinist; even the
word "California" could be highly charged to some
people. She knew it was a country apart, so she could
afford to be offhand about mentioning it.

"Spring is great anywhere," she said, letting her blue-
gray eyes speak for her. "See," they said, "I can be
friendly."

"Don't get your hopes up. This is a freak. We'll probably have a couple of blizzards and snowfalls yet."
Exactly what Lorene had said.

And how long were they going to go on about the
weather? Elizabeth stopped for a second; she had something important to say.

"I want to tell you, Dan, that speech you gave in
assembly today was terrific. I was really impressed."

True. She was impressed with his brilliance when he
spoke about American relations with Asia. His eyes had
blazed as he spoke out about things that would not be
popular with many of the students or even the faculty.
So he had courage too. He ducked his head with mock
boyishness at the compliment.

"Well, thank you, Liz. I didn't know you ever listened
to anyone."

4

"That's unfair. I do. More than you think."

They had come to the corner, and there they stopped. Two little girls rushing by on roller skates would have bumped into them, but they both stepped back in time. He grinned at her, and she thought he looked about to ask her to go walking perhaps or to have a Coke with him. He hesitated, then spoke decisively.

"Sorry, Liz, but I've got to split. Have to meet someone on the paper. It's been good seeing you again."

"You too," she nodded understandingly and watched him stride down the street. Without looking back. After the tiniest of sighs, she started for Lorene's. Now the housewives really seemed to be gossiping and Elizabeth sensed malice in it. Nor did they speak kindly to their children. One yelled, "Hey, Joey, get outta the road or I'll smack you one."

The world turned bleak and unpleasant once more. "I don't belong here. I'll never belong here."

Two blocks later she was in front of Lorene's. "Now I want you-all to think of this as home, yoah home from now on, y'heah?' Lorene had said when, after the marriage, their father had brought them to Lorene's house with promises of a larger place later on.

"I'll never think of it as home. Never," Elizabeth had told Mark. Her brother was only twelve, but he had become her closest and practically her only friend, except for Patty. But did Patty really count? She still belonged to Lorene. And Lorene was the enemy.

Elizabeth had to admit grudgingly that Lorene had been genuinely gracious, but still it was *Lorene's* home, and ugly besides. A tract house painted a practical tan that wouldn't show the dirt — Lorene herself had been proud of her foresight — a sentimental house with a rose bush around the front door, which Elizabeth

5

prophesied would put out a bounty of thorns and only a few stingy blossoms. American flag decals pasted in every window in front of the white ruffled curtains. A plastic Bambi lawn ornament. How could her father have let himself in for all this? A temporary derangement.

As she started up the front walk, Elizabeth heard Lorene giving a piano lesson. Her voice with its indefinite southern accent mingled with the stumbling march and soured the afternoon.

"Rest, two, three, foah! Rest, two, three, foah! Bobbie Jo, you can do bettah than that! Now let's trah it again. Count now! One, two —"

Elizabeth walked around to the back of the house, but instead of going to the room she shared with Patty, she went to Mark's room. Lucky Mark! Their father had built him a room on the far side of the garage away from the house. Mark wasn't there, but Elizabeth's records and record player were. She put on a record that Rick had given her, kicked off her shoes, and lay down on Mark's bed. The record was almost worn out by now, it had been played so much, but still she shut her eyes and let the music roll over her.

The first time she'd heard it, she had been lying by Rick's pool in the late lime-yellow sun of an August afternoon. She saw herself, honey-tanned in a white bikini, and Rick, Ken and Linda sitting around and listening, all of them feeling a harmony such as they'd never felt before. She told herself then, and she believed it now, that she had never been so happy.

"If Rick asks me to marry him when I go home instead of waiting —" the possibility had occurred to her several times, shocking at first, because she was only sixteen, but more and more appealing each time she thought about it. It was understood that they were serious about each other, and Rick's parents liked her well enough, particularly Rick's father. Getting married now would solve so many problems — like never having to live with Lorene again.

"I'll write to Rick," she thought, "not about the marriage, of course, but to keep in touch." Rick had answered her many letters only once, but she forgave him. Some people did not write easily.

She found paper on Mark's desk and, perched on his bed, began the letter: "Dear Rick,"

What was there to say? She bit the end of her pen and tried to recall his face. She knew he had dark hair and that his eyebrows met in the middle, but try as she might, she couldn't remember the details of his face, and that, she realized, was odd, because she remembered perfectly, in every detail, the little red Porsche. She tore up the letter and went to her own room. She'd write later, when she was in the mood.

# 2

Winter made a chilling comeback. On Thursday, a cold sunless day, something nagged at Elizabeth. A birthday? An anniversary of some sort? She couldn't remember. That night at dinner, while Lorene called to Patty to bring in the mashed potatoes and urged her father to "take some moah po'k chops. I sweah, the price keeps goin' up and up," — her father never could stand hearing about it while he ate — Elizabeth noticed that he seemed more quiet than usual. Then she remembered. It *was* an anniversary. Only a year ago that day, a year that seemed a century, her own mother had come home from court, the divorce having just been completed.

Her mother had walked into the house slowly, looking beaten and dazed; she might have been acting one of her favorite roles, the deserted woman in a gloomy Irish play. Friends would have said, "Wouldn't you know, that's just like Mollie!" But it was too sad to be a joke.

"I've got the headache bad, Elizabeth. I think I'll take to bed."

Elizabeth had brought her a pot of tea and, when she had asked for it, the whiskey. She had stood there silently while her mother poured a generous touch into the tea. And what if her mother became an alcoholic now? Good Lord, what's happening to all of us, Elizabeth had asked herself again and again. Everything's falling apart.

She found herself judging her mother as her father would have done, sternly and smugly. *It's your own fault, Mother, carrying on with that idiot. You know Dad doesn't stand for that kind of thing, but he can't help it. That's how he is — straight. Uncompromising. You should have known that.*

Yet she was very like her mother, and when Elizabeth saw her lying there sad-eyed and dreary under the covers, she longed to comfort her. *"Poor Mom!" It's all over now. We all make mistakes, but it's not the end. Everything will be better tomorrow, you just wait and see. It might all be for the best after all. Who knows? Try to get some sleep now, that's a good girl."*

In the end, she had only stood there and said nothing. She wondered what her father was doing, alone in his bare apartment. Nobody had died, but there was a feeling of death in the air, as though something dear was gone forever. Later, when her mother fell asleep, Elizabeth went downstairs and made dinner for Mark and her little sister, Penny, who was only five and didn't understand why Daddy wasn't coming home. Nobody ate anything.

The next week her mother was offered a good role in a play, and she came to life once more, throwing herself into the part with desperate enthusiasm. Elizabeth was relieved that her mother would not become a lush after all. In time a new gentleman, a fiftyish businessman, began to come around, and Mark and Elizabeth, now close allies, felt themselves in the way. Their father had taken on a job in Lincoln, since he couldn't bear to live in Sacramento any more. As soon as school was out, they had gone to join him, promising their tearful mother they'd be back the next year and hoping she would beg them to stay. But she didn't.

The first few months with their father in an apartment with a minimum of furnishings had been fun, a little like camping or playing house. . . .

"Cat got yoah tongue, Elizabeth? Dahlin', you eat like a bird. Trah the apple buttah on the biscuits. Ah'll bet they don' have apple buttah like this in Califo'nia. C'mon now, honey."

"Thanks. I'm not hungry." Elizabeth found poison in Lorene's sweetness. How could she be anything but icy toward the woman who tried to take her mother's place?

9

"Ah sweah," Lorene continued, "everyone looks and acts so gloomy tonight. Whát *is* the mattah? Oh Liz, deah, Ah almost forgot! You got a package today in the mail."

A package! Maybe something from Rick? Dinner was taking forever with Lorene's "babies," Cissie and L'il Joey, clamoring for more pudding. At last Lorene gave her the package. She caressed the I. Magnin label and the California postmark before opening it and found a dress from her mother and a card in her sloppy, generous handwriting: "Thinking of you, darling. Love. Mother." Later when she was alone, she would kiss the card.

She held up the dress from its tissue wrappings, while Patty looked on and let out her breath with an admiring "oh." The sigh of a ten-year-old little sister. And it was a splendid dress with enough suggestion of Chinese influence to make it exotic without being freakish.

"Try it on, Elizabeth! I can't wait to see you in it. Ooooh, it's so beautiful!"

Patty, squealing with pleasure, followed Elizabeth to her room, and even Elizabeth's face, usually pale, was rosy with excitement. It had been a long time since she'd had a new dress, and knowing that her mother chose it for her made it all the more precious. What an instinct her mother had for fashion and fine things! Lorene, in her navy blue suit with the glittering American flag pin over her heart, could not possibly understand. But Patty was still sighing over it.

"You're so *lucky*, Liz. You're so *beautiful!* Can I have that dress when it gets old and you don't want it any more?"

"You're not so bad yourself, Patty," Elizabeth said to her admirer. Patty is right, she thought, looking at her-

10

self in the mirror. Her beauty was tall and restrained, at the moment a bit pale, but once back in California she would tan easily enough. Her mother's friends were always asking why she didn't pose for *Vogue* or *Seventeen*. Well, being lovely didn't solve problems, but it was better than looking like Lorene, say, or poor Patty, whose paleness was like that of cornstarch pudding and who would someday have to fight a dumpy look like her mother's. Yet Patty's eyes, behind the glasses, had a brightness and sparkle that made Elizabeth think she might turn out all right after all. Elizabeth turned again to admire herself.

She showed the dress to her father, who nodded his approval and smiled, the first time all evening. Mark whistled.

Lorene was the discordant note. "Ah suppose they weah things like that in Califo'nia, but it's pretty garish for aroun' heah. And it's too sho't, honey, way too sho't. Let me look at the hem. Good! You could let it down two inches, Liz."

"I like it exactly the way it is," she said, although ten minutes before she had wondered if she should lengthen it a little. She looked to her father for support.

"Really, Chahles, Liz is a young lady now. It's hardly decent, not aroun' here."

"All right, Liz, you heard what Lorene said. She knows about these things."

"But, Dad . . ."

"Be a good girl now. Do what she says. Fix that hem."

His eyes lowered to the engineering journal he was reading, as if the matter were settled. Too big to stamp her foot or shout back, too stubborn to show her resentment toward Lorene, she went to her room quietly.

11

There she closed the door and leaned against it, biting her lip to keep from crying out. That bitch! The woman who was supposed to replace her mother! Tears of anger filled her eyes as she took out her sewing kit. She longed for her mother, a longing filled with pain.

She took off the dress, sat on the edge of the bed, and began to pull out the hem, then stopped as a slow smile came to her lips. She would change the hemline, all right, by taking it *up* two inches! The dress really would be indecent now, she felt, but with opaque tights it might be forgivable. She had never fought a grown woman before. In fact, she had never fought with anyone. But Lorene was an enemy, and she would no longer pretend it wasn't so.

The next morning Elizabeth went down to breakfast, after her father had left for work. When she appeared in the shortened dress, her long legs looking longer and slimmer than ever, Lorene shrieked with anger. Elizabeth sipped her orange juice calmly, hardly seeming to listen.

"Ah give up. You are *impossible*. An ungrateful child. All Ah can say is yoah father deserves bettah from you. It's a good thing he hasn't seen what you did to that dress. Now you go upstairs lak a good girl and take that hem down and Ah promise Ah won't say a word about it."

But Elizabeth pretended not to hear her. She finished her toast and coffee in silence, and without even looking at Lorene, put on her jacket, picked up her books, and went off to school.

# 3

Victory had its price. The few girls who had stared at Elizabeth's dress had not admired it. Boys had stared at it too, but she had a reputation for being unapproachable, so it did not encourage them. The trouble with a short dress was not its indecency as much as its coldness. She was chilly all day and changed to wool pants and a sweater when she got home, forgetting about the dress.

Lorene, however, was not one to forget a slight. All day her anger had bubbled, and at dinner she threw meaningful looks at Elizabeth as she said, "Ah've got somethin' to tell you, Chahles, but it'll keep until after the puddin'."

"Oh God," Elizabeth groaned under her breath and Mark kicked her under the table. Once before Lorene had heard her say it and had lectured for twenty minutes about "takin' the name of the Lo'd in vain."

Dinner as always was too long, with her father silent and Lorene talking, complaints and childish squealings from four-year-old Cissie, and L'il Joe, unpleasant even at two, a little boy with a nose that always seemed to need wiping.

What was wrong with Lorene anyway, Elizabeth wondered as she toyed with the food on her plate. Lorene wasn't such a bad-looking woman — not like her own mother, of course, but still, aside from a certain dumpiness, conventionally pretty. She might have posed for a TV commercial for floorwax, or brighter dentures, or the cleaner washing powder that would solve the most pressing problem of every woman's life. Yet Lorene wasn't stupid.

"What's wrong," Mark had said and Elizabeth had agreed, "is that it's impossible to like her." When Lorene was most objectionable, they referred to her as the Black Widow. She truly had been a widow when their father first took her out, and they had joked about it. Yet Elizabeth wondered if the comparison were entirely unjust. What *was* Lorene doing to their father?

After dinner, the little ones went to watch TV, but Patty, who guessed what was coming, remained at the table and looked at Elizabeth with sympathy. "I'm on your side," her eyes flashed. Lorene prepared for battle.

"Elizabeth, tell yoah father what you did to your new dress."

Elizabeth looked at her father without flinching. "I shortened it two inches and wore it to school that way."

The TV, which had been blastingly loud up to this time, turned to sudden silence as the two little ones came back to look at Elizabeth. A better show was going on here, a struggle even they could feel. Was Elizabeth going to get a licking, big as she was? A vein throbbed in her father's forehead, and he looked utterly weary as he let his journal drop to the floor. Elizabeth's eyes lowered in guilt; she did not mean to make so much trouble for him.

"Get your coat, Liz. We'll take a ride. I want to talk with you."

Elizabeth got her coat, threw it carelessly over her shoulders, winked at Patty, and left with her father. A temporary victory, she was cheating Lorene from observing a scolding from her father. He drove out to the edge of the park and pulled over to the curb. The stars twinkled fiercely in the chill dark night and the wind whipped against the car. Elizabeth put on her coat, wrapping it tightly around her, and shivering, snuggled against her father. He took a pipe from his pocket, filled it, lit it, and took a deep satisfying draught.

"It's such a good smell. I've been missing it," Elizabeth said. Her father never smoked at Lorene's, for although she did not forbid it, every time he took out his pipe, she lectured about cancer.

"Dad, let's leave Lorene. It's such a mess there. Then you, Mark and I can live together the way we used to. I'll really learn to cook, I promise. We were happy before, weren't we?"

"In a way."

It had been a little like camping, living in that small apartment. Elizabeth, finding herself a nest-maker, drew plans and sketches for the furniture they would buy when there was enough money. But when her cooking fell short of perfection — a hard spot in the center of a potato or an overbaked chicken — her father would frown and take them all out to a restaurant.

Worse than that had been his preoccupied silences. She and Mark became the parents and he the child with the problem. They tried to amuse him and even encouraged him to go out with women. They had joked together about the Black Widow with the little round bottom that wiggled when she walked, but if she kept him company, surely it was all right. But marriage? With that one? When his intentions became clear, Elizabeth had become tearful and begged him not to marry her, begged him again and again until he stormed at her. In the end she and Mark, white with foreboding, had stood in the minister's study, looking unhappily at Lorene's three children, while her father slipped the ring on his new wife's finger.

"About Lorene, Dad," Elizabeth explained four months later as they sat in the car on a freezing night. "Mother, *my* mother, sent me the dress. Lorene didn't go out and buy it. Or anything else. I'm good at home. I don't talk back to her. I do the dishes. In school my grades are good. I even baby-sit free. What more does that excuse-for-a-woman want from me?"

"Don't get abusive, Liz. I wasn't going to scold you. You don't have it too easy; I know that. Let's put it this way. It's not easy for someone like Lorene to live with a beauti — well, a good-looking young girl."

"Stepmothers in fairy stories are always wicked. It must be because it's true in life. She is."

"Not really, Liz. She's very different from you. She knows you dislike her, even when she tries to be pleasant. You're smarter than she is and you come from California, which makes some people resentful, though God knows why. I don't. To have a sixteen-year-old daughter thrust on you suddenly isn't the easiest thing in the world."

"But how could you have *married* her, Dad? And after Mother, too. Mother may do dumb things sometime, but she's a real woman. Okay, so Lorene is neater, for heaven's sake, as if that mattered, but you know that Mom has never in her life been mean or small or spiteful. If I'd run off and married someone, you'd have annulled it just like that. But when you do something ridiculous . . ."

"Come now, Liz. At the time I did what seemed best

and most important. Damn it, girl, nobody ever said you know all the answers just because your hair is getting thin. You did need . . . you still need . . . a mother. So does Mark. And just possibly I need a wife."

"We were happier without her. Just the three of us."

"And in another year, Liz, you'll be going off to college. Mark will follow a few years later. I wanted a real home for you."

"You call that place a home?"

"Give her a chance, Liz. She has a good heart, really. And she's decent. And she does like music."

Like music! Elizabeth was about to say something about that too, but held her tongue. Music was her father's weakness, her father's love. How many times she had come upon him listening, concentrating, really hearing the Bach cello sonatas or Mozart quartets or the quintet he loved more than anything else, so engrossed he did not even realize she was there! So how could he endure Lorene whose favorite composer was Tchaikovsky, Lorene who played *None But the Lonely Heart* with so many runs and flourishes that it was all she and Mark could do to keep from laughing? No, it wasn't music that brought them together. The only possible explanation was that he had been out of his mind with grief after the divorce and not responsible.

"Anyway, Liz, I want to ask one thing of you, please," he said, looking at her directly. "Be good to Lorene. Try to get along with her. Don't giggle with Mark as if you had secrets; she thinks you're laughing at her, and it hurts her. You'll be leaving in June, so it's only for a little while longer. So for my sake, will you fix the dress and get along with her?"

He was a proud man, and Elizabeth would have preferred the authoritarian tone he sometimes used to this pleading. She knew it wasn't easy for him to ask for favors.

"All right, I'll try. I promise," she said, and oddly enough she felt relieved. He had not asked her to like Lorene or consider her a mother, but only to live with her in peace for the next few months.

She kissed her father's cheek and rested her head on his shoulder. They sat that way for several minutes and then, because the cold was too penetrating, he started the car and they went home.

Although she said goodnight to Lorene pleasantly enough, that night she dreamed Lorene was chasing her with a hatchet to the edge of a precipice. Patty shook Elizabeth's shoulders and rescued her from the nightmare in the nick of time. Elizabeth, shivering, held her and thanked her. After staring into the darkness for a long time, she finally fell asleep.

# 4

From that night on Elizabeth suffered nightmares, something that had never happened before. Her dreams which, in the past, had been lyrical, gently sad and sometimes amusing, not unlike a movie played for her enjoyment, had changed to visions of such violence she was almost afraid to go to sleep. The kindest nightmare of them all found her tied to a jet taking off to a distant planet, never to return, waving to Lorene as she disappeared. More disturbing was the time she dreamed she had finished drinking a glass of milk, only to find Lorene grinning crazily and telling her she had put poison in it. In other dreams Lorene chased Elizabeth down the streets of Lincoln with a knife or tied her to a stake and lit fires around her. More than once Patty had shaken Elizabeth awake and thrown her arms around her to comfort her.

"I'll sleep with you if you like," she promised, her face full of concern. "Then you won't have such bad dreams."

"Patty, you're so nice," Elizabeth had whispered, still trembling from the nightmare. She longed to tell someone about her dreams and be reassured, but Lorene's daughter was hardly the one to confide in, so she sent her back to bed.

"I'll be all right now. Don't tell anyone, will you, Patty? It must have been something I had for dinner."

Oddly enough she was getting along much better with Lorene, avoiding her as before, but being helpful and polite as she had promised her father she would be. And so the growing fierceness of the nightmares puzzled her more than ever.

"If I don't tell anyone, maybe they'll just go away," she decided. Still they came, sometimes two and three in a single night. And June was farther away than ever.

# 5

March seemed endless, but April came at last. One morning Elizabeth found a note on her desk in school that told her she had an appointment with Miss

Gretchen Isham — known by students as "Stretch and itch-em" — the school counselor and psychologist, at three that afternoon. Immediately Elizabeth was suspicious. What did she want?

Lorene had sometimes mentioned Miss Isham, whom she had met when she substituted as a teacher in the high school. Immediately, the suspicion that Lorene was using Miss Isham to get rid of her occurred to Elizabeth. It seemed curiously like her nightmares.

"Am I paranoid?" she asked herself as she waited in Miss Isham's office. A pleasant room in clear yellow and blues, with good teak furniture, hand-blocked linen drapes and Japanese woodcuts on the walls. Miss Isham had good taste. Then what could she possibly have to do with someone like Lorene? Elizabeth decided the best thing to do was to say as little as possible until she knew.

Ten minutes after the scheduled appointment time, when Elizabeth was on the verge of leaving, a tall woman tripped in. "Trip" was the right word because she seemed on the verge of falling over the threshold.

"I'm late, late, late, late, late!" she repeated like a character in a child's musical comedy. "I'm sorry, Elizabeth. Hope you didn't mind waiting." A little strange perhaps, but pleasant, Elizabeth decided.

"It's all right."

Miss Isham's smile was immediate and genuine. She might have been forty or so, but the awkwardness of an adolescent who had grown up too fast clung to her, a charming clumsiness. The vague blue eyes magnified behind thick-lensed glasses, like fish trapped in an aquarium, focused on Elizabeth, who wondered if she were being admired. It was not so much a matter of being conceited as much as having seen just such a look on the faces of many girls and women she had met. They were looks that could be either admiring, jealous or wistful. Miss Isham had the wistful look, like that of a sixteen-year-old girl or one even younger, like Patty. Maybe Miss Isham was not entirely grown up.

Elizabeth often felt too much fuss was made about people looking beautiful or attractive. It was never worth either the envy or the wistfulness. Once she herself had been jealous of a folk singer, a girl with a long nose and stringy hair, because when that girl sang, her magic was worth more than anyone's good looks. Elizabeth suffered other shortcomings, that she did not sing, nor did she dance or ski well, or do any of the things she admired.

Nobody ever thought about the responsibility of being a pretty girl. She had to watch her posture because tall people tended to stoop. She could never eat as much chocolate as she craved. And what a problem she had with colors! Anything too brilliant washed her out, and she faded with a dress that was too pale. Another girl wouldn't have had to be so careful.

"Well, Elizabeth," Miss Isham said, looking up from the file she had been reading. Her eyes, no longer vague or wistful, became direct. X-ray eyes. Elizabeth caught the look and remembered to be careful about what she said, so that she wouldn't walk into any traps.

"Do you like living in Lincoln?"

"It's all right, I suppose."

"Not very exciting, I imagine. And chilly, after California." Miss Isham's smile was sympathetic. "Your grades are excellent; only one person — you do know Daniel Wilson, don't you? — ranks higher. That's very

21

good, Elizabeth, because the transcript from Sacramento shows a much lower grade average. Maybe you find this school that much easier?"

"Not really. I work harder."

"Do you find it interesting here?"

Elizabeth shrugged her shoulders as though it didn't matter. "Not necessarily. Studying makes the time go faster, that's all."

"That's *all*?"

It would never do to confess that she, who had never cared about marks before, now found it amusing, almost satisfying, to get good grades. Not unlike the satisfaction of winning games or races. And if the students thought her a snob because she had never gone to their parties or played their games, the high grades did give her something to be snobbish about. Suddenly, at that moment, her reason seemed so petty that she realized it wasn't the real one at all.

"Doesn't it give you any satisfaction to be outstanding?"

"I couldn't care less." Her voice sounded more insolent than Elizabeth intended, and not wanting to appear the difficult adolescent, she spoke more warmly. "It's only a game. Actually, it's mechanical. You put in study; you take out good grades. If I had something more worthwhile to do, I'd do it and let the grades go."

"What would something 'better' be?"

"Going back to California."

"That's a place. You'd still have to find something better 'to do,' wouldn't you?"

This Miss Isham was sharp. "Whatever I find to do, I'll find there," Elizabeth answered.

"The important thing, Elizabeth, is to find something that has meaning for you. I'm sure you must have many talents. Discovering one of them might make all the difference in the world. I've often wondered if you liked acting. I hear your mother is an actress."

Where did she hear that, Elizabeth wondered. Did such information get into the records? How much else did she know?

"I detest acting," she found herself saying. It was true, but she herself was surprised at how emphatic she made it sound. "My mother is a semi-professional actress in a small resident company, that's all. As for me, I loathe being in the spotlight."

"Many people do," Mis Isham sympathized. Elizabeth was beginning to think Lorene had not been in touch with her after all, but she was still cautious. "What do you like to do?"

"All I want to do is to go back to Sacramento. Then I suppose I'll do what I did before. See my friends, go swimming, go to the mountains, ride around. There were four of us together, and all we ever needed was each other."

"It sounds pleasant enough. I suppose you write to them and can't wait to get their letters."

Miss Isham had put her finger (an innocent finger?) on the sore spot. Elizabeth's seven- and ten-page letters had been answered by two short notes from Linda, a card from Ken and not much more from Rick.

"I guess they're too busy to write. Not everyone enjoys writing. Anyway, it's not necessary, because we have *faith* in each other," she ended triumphantly.

"So that's why you never joined the clubs here or took part in anything at school? A kind of loyalty perhaps? I hear you were immensely popular the first few weeks of school."

"Everyone was very friendly and kind, that's true.

But there wasn't any sense in my getting involved. You see, I'll be going back soon. In June."

"I see. But you'll be back for your senior year, won't you? Perhaps it might be a good idea to get involved. Not all the clubs here are that bad."

"Miss Isham, if my mother lets me stay with her, I will never come back here."

She stopped in confusion, realizing that she had taken for granted that her mother would want to keep her, but at that moment the "if" she had used proved to her that she wasn't entirely sure of this. Then she'd have to spend still another year with Lorene. The horror of it made her feel faint.

"Is there something wrong, Elizabeth?"

"No, not really."

"Something is bothering you, isn't it?"

The eyes spoke kindness, and Elizabeth was alarmed to feel the sting of tears in her own, for she seldom wept. Her father had never been able to stand crying and she had learned restraint early. She longed to tell Miss Isham about Lorene and the nightmares and to ask how she could stop them because they were getting worse all the time. But she was afraid of what Miss Isham might say or even more of what Miss Isham might do.

"If you want to talk about it, maybe that will help."

Elizabeth was about to say yes, but someone knocked on the door.

"Oh dear," Miss Isham said, standing up. "I'm sorry, Elizabeth, but I do have another appointment and it's already late. If you want to see me about anything at all, I'll be here. Just make an appointment with the secretary. All right, dear?"

24

"Thanks very much."

Miss Isham held out her hand and smiled a smile that said to Elizabeth: hold on, take courage.

Courage? She would need it. The interview had stirred up too many ghosts and she no longer felt certain about anything, only that June was too long in coming.

# 6

As Elizabeth approached the house, she could hear Lorene having difficulties with Cissie and L'il Joe, who were squealing at each other while she tried to give a piano lesson.

"Patty's gone off somewheah and the little ones are bein' devils," Lorene told her, obviously distressed.

Elizabeth offered to take them to the park.

"Would you, Liz? You can be such a darlin' when you want to be."

As Elizabeth helped Cissie on the swings and wiped L'il Joe's nose, she realized this was a sacrifice of a few hours, a bargain with the gods, for which she begged a night without nightmares. Her offering was far from stingy. She bought ice cream for the children and wiped their chins when the cream dribbled down. No, she did not like Cissie, could not stand L'il Joe, and wondered why adults were supposed to love all children. Already she could see what charmless adults they would become, and this feeling made her favor to Lorene seem all the more significant.

Elizabeth's elaborate appeasement to the gods was in vain. That night brought the most violent and garish dream she had had yet. Lorene lay murdered on the flowered rug in the living room, blood spreading everywhere, while her eyes, not yet dead, followed Elizabeth accusingly. Elizabeth hadn't murdered her, and she cried, "I didn't do it!" But the eyes followed her just the same. She ran to the door, found it was locked, and banged on it with both fists, until at last it swung open. She fled in giant steps to Sacramento. More shock awaited her there, for the city had been reduced to one vast area of rubble as far as the eye could see. An earthquake, a bomb or some other catastrophe had destroyed it. Bridges had been broken and highway overpasses stood on end pointing to the sky. Yet portions of homes were left untouched; walls had been torn away to show tidy breakfast rooms with coffee still perking in percolators and frothy white curtains stirring gently. Smoke drifted upward from piles of broken walls and overturned cars. Only the arches of a McDonald's stand rose above the ruins, a tribute to a lost civilization. Horrified, Elizabeth walked among the ruins, the wind blowing her hair. "Isn't anybody here?" her voice echoed and re-echoed, and at last she knew she was alone, the only one left alive.

"Wake up, Liz, wake up now!" Patty's face peering into her own reflected Elizabeth's terror. "It's all right now, Liz. You're here."

Elizabeth moaned like someone coming out of an anesthetic. This had been the worst dream yet and not easy to shake. She hugged Patty thankfully and drew her toward her as she sat up in bed.

"Poor Liz! That must have been an awful one. What

was it like?" Patty whispered, and when Elizabeth could only shake her head, she asked, "Want me to get you some warm milk or somethin'?"

"No, it's all right," she said as soon as the trembling stopped. "You're sweet, Patty, such a sweet kid, really. I shouldn't be waking you up every night like this."

"I don't mind, Liz. I'm so glad to have you here. You're different, you know?"

"Do you ever dream anything, Patty?"

Patty giggled and put her hand over her mouth. "Sure, but not like your dreams. I can't tell you," she whispered and giggled some more, while Elizabeth smiled indulgently. How nice it must be to be ten years old and able to giggle like that!

After Patty went back to her own bed, Elizabeth peered into the dark, trying to understand the nightmare. Did she actually hate Lorene that much? That violently? She considered how she actually did feel, as honestly as she could, and with relief found that although she did not like Lorene, she did not hate her. Certainly she wished her no harm. So why the violent dreams? And what did all that about Sacramento in ruins really mean?

For the first time the suspicion came to her as she lay wide-eyed in the dark, that Lorene was only a focus on the surface, hiding a deeper, more serious restlessness that Elizabeth felt but could not recognize. A vision of something unseen stirring under dark waters.

"I'm scared!" she said to herself as she burrowed under the covers. She was afraid to go to sleep again. If only someone could help her . . .

Miss Isham? Of course. Miss Isham had offered to help her. Maybe all she needed was someone to talk with. Surely Miss Isham, more than anyone else, would help her to understand her fears. First thing in the morning she would make an appointment to see her.

Already feeling better, she fell into a sound, dreamless sleep.

# 7

"Dad, you'd really like Buffy Ste. Marie. Please, could we go? I'd love to see her again. Remember, I had all those records of hers?"

Several weeks before her talk with Miss Isham, Elizabeth had seen a poster announcing that Buffy Ste. Marie would be giving a concert in Lincoln. This stirred up memories of her mother taking her to hear Buffy in San Francisco when Elizabeth was eight and later, because both of them loved the Indian singer, going into a record store and extravagantly buying several albums. Elizabeth, looking back, saw herself sitting on the floor and playing the records over and over until they wore thin. She had gone on to other kinds of music, but Buffy Ste. Marie was always very special, the singer she liked most. Hearing her would be like going back to her childhood again.

Her father understood. He smiled indulgently and stroked her smooth hair. "The original Buffy fan! Of course you can go, Liz. Here, is this enough for a ticket?" He took out his wallet and gave her a five-dollar bill.

"But I want you to come too."

"I'm afraid not, sweetie. I don't think Lorene would care for it. But I'm glad you want to go. And I do think she's a fine singer. By the way, if you hear about any concert of Beethoven string quartets coming up, I'll be happy to take you. Right?"

His eyes twinkled, and for that Elizabeth hugged him, smiling herself. The reference to a Beethoven concert was a lame family joke. When Elizabeth was a little girl, her father had promised to take her to a concert. Without the faintest idea of what a concert might be, she had boasted to her friends how she would be all dressed up and how her father would take her to Blum's afterward for ice cream. Yet the concert proved to be torture. She had squirmed through the first quartet and slept during the remaining two, leaning against her father. The final burst of applause woke her and she asked her father when the concert would begin. "You mean all they did was play music?" she had asked, in bitter disappointment. But that was long ago.

"I might surprise you yet," Elizabeth said, "and be glad to listen to a Beethoven quartet. But come and hear Buffy with me, please? Lorene can stay home by herself for one night, can't she?"

"Another time, pet. We're still 'adjusting,' you know. Maybe Mark would like to go."

"He's got band rehearsals on Thursday nights."

She bought the ticket for herself, and on Thursday morning begged him again to go with her that night. He said no, but praised her. "You've been fine toward Lorene, Liz. I've been watching you, and I appreciate it. So this is a promise, I'll take you to the next concert. Okay?"

29

That afternoon she ran a long warm bath. Her father had noticed that not once had she exchanged a knowing wink with Mark or groaned "Oh God!" or otherwise offended Lorene. Her father seemed happier now. If it weren't for the nightmares, she would hold out until June after all.

"You still in theah, Liz? That's a mighty long bath," Lorene had yelled through the door. She had once complained, "Ah jus' can't understand why you like to bathe so much. Hours and hours."

Elizabeth poured in more hot water and lay back, dreaming. That night she would see Buffy Ste. Marie. The next day at three she would see Miss Isham, who would understand what was wrong, and then the nightmares would stop. June would come in no time at all. Again she saw herself walking from the plane to the waiting room, and this time Rick had an extravagant bouquet of flowers for her, and they would go off in his car and, of course, then she would know exactly what he looked like, even if she couldn't remember now. She saw them driving up to the mountains and lying in the sun, the scent of pines close by.

As she got out of the tub and dried herself, she noticed how pale she had become. "Ugh, like a mushroom," she said. Soon she would take long sunbaths to bring back the warm honey color, and she saw herself in a new white bikini and later a bareback white dress. New sandals. But for the moment she was glad to put on the dress her mother had sent.

"Well, look who's all dressed up. You were in that bath over an hour, Liz. You goin' somewhere?" Lorene asked at dinner as she passed the noodle casserole.

30

Elizabeth took a scant spoonful, fearing what it would do to her figure, and longed for a green salad.

"I'm going to the Buffy Ste. Marie concert, Lorene. Remember, I told you about it when I bought the ticket?"

"Not rilly. Honey, your fathah and I are goin' out tonight. You knew that now, didn't you? It's a special party for the church choir."

"So?"

"I was expectin' you would baby-sit. After all, you nevah do go anywhere. I didn't know about this concert."

"Why can't Patty do it?"

"Patty's just a child. And she ought to be in bed. She's got a cold."

"I don' mind, Mom," Patty spoke up, finishing in a burst of coughing.

"You see?" Lorene proved her point.

Elizabeth's father seemed to be concentrating very hard on the casserole as though he didn't want to be involved.

"I guess you did say somethin' about a concert, but I thought it was tomorrow. Well, I'll go call some high school girls now and see if they can come. L'il Joe, get your fingers out of the plate."

Lorene went to the kitchen to telephone while Elizabeth, waiting, tore her napkin to shreds. Old fears began to crowd in. After several calls, Lorene returned.

"Well, Ah've called about everyone I know. Guess what's goin' on tonight? Unbelievable! A game, a dramatic club play, band rehearsal and everyone that's not goin' to those places is goin' to a good movie. Ah'd be glad to stay home, but Ah promised to make presentations and accompany the soloist, and besides I want to introduce yoah fathah, Liz. Everyone's been dyin' to meet him. Don't you have a girl frien', could sit for you?"

Elizabeth's eyes flashed at her father for help. He cleared his throat.

"Lorene, I think I'd better stay home. We should have had our signals straight but we didn't. So count me out this time and I'll meet your choir on another occasion."

Good Daddy! He was on her side. Elizabeth sat up straighter now.

"But Chahles, I've been lookin' forward to this too, just as much as Elizabeth wants to go to her concert. You cain't disappoint everyone like that. It's not just that I want to have a selfish time listenin' to a concert. I promised to be there and I promised to bring you. They'll think something is funny if you don't come. Elizabeth can go to a concert any ole time."

Yes, Dad, what about that? Elizabeth waited, becoming taut as a stretched string. What her father did now was of the utmost importance. There was a battle after all, and he had to make the choice, Lorene or her. What he might have said was interrupted as Cissie turned on the TV full force, and L'il Joe yelled that he wanted his channel. Lorene settled that matter, and in the moment she was gone, her father made his decision.

"Well, honey, I'm in a tight spot over this. In the future we'll have to mesh our plans or write down our dates so we don't get mixed up. Elizabeth, I really did promise Lorene I'd go with her. This affair means a lot to her. Can we get you another ticket for tomorrow night?"

"No. She's here for only one concert," Elizabeth said, her voice becoming high and tight.

"Oh dear. Well, I'll make it up to you. First, we'll get some new records for you, and I promise I'll take you to the very next concert you want to go to. All right?"

"No." Elizabeth shook her head.

It was a quiet, uncompromising "no," and the coolness of it and Elizabeth's direct look, combined with the blare of the TV from the other room, tore down her father's attempt at diplomacy. The nerve in his forehead throbbed and his voice became taut and angry.

"It's time you listened to some decent music anyway. The trash you listen to in Mark's room is unspeakably bad, bad in every way. When are you going to grow up?"

Elizabeth gazed at him without moving while he shouted at her. He used to shout at her mother in just such an illogical way when he was clearly the one at fault. "It's just frustration," her mother had explained. "Just wait it out, let it fall like water off a duck's back. You might as well fight a thunderstorm when he's like that," was another way her mother had put it. So Elizabeth waited, but at the same time another decision, something entirely new, a remarkable and frightening idea was forming itself in Elizabeth's mind. Fascinated with it, she let it happen without trying to stop it.

"Please, Elizabeth, just this once. Ah would appreciate it so much and Ah'll make it up to you too. Ah'll take you to a real good concert."

Without smiling and without a single word, Elizabeth stood up and began to clear the table. Patty helped. "Gee, aren't you gonna hear Buffy Ste. Marie?" she asked, almost as disappointed as Elizabeth.

"I guess not. Don't worry, Patty. There are other things to do."

She ran upstairs, changed into jeans, and went downstairs again. She might as well do the dishes while she waited.

"Smile, honey, come on, let's see a smile. You look so pretty when you smile. We won't evah forget this, Liz. You're a real good spo't."

No smile, no tears, only a cool appraising look from the steady gray eyes that Elizabeth knew would have wilted any woman more sensitive than Lorene. It was a look that took in the new pink suit, the cheap perfume that was too strong, and the self-satisfied curl of Lorene's lips. Elizabeth wondered, and then gave up wondering forever, why her father should have chosen such a woman. He stood beside her, self-righteous, ready to leave. He nodded at Elizabeth as though she had been the one who had lost her temper and it was he who forgave her.

"Take care," he said.

Unsmiling still, she watched them leave and did not move until the door was shut behind them.

"It's the last I'll see of them," she said.

Then she went to finish the dishes.

# 8

The children were neither better nor worse than usual. They fought over which TV program they wanted to watch and Patty sat at the kitchen table, biting her fingers as she read a library book. When she became involved in a book, she neither heard nor saw anything else that might be going on around her. But she stopped long enough to watch Elizabeth drying the last of the pots.

"Watcha gonna do about it, Liz?"

"Do about what?" Elizabeth answered cautiously, as she decided she would make the goodnight cocoa for the little ones now and get them out of the way. It was early, but fortunately they couldn't tell time.

"You know," Patty was persistent. "You're thinking up something, aren't you? I can tell."

A bright one, that Patty. Someday, Elizabeth could almost see it, that girl would grow up, light out of that house in a snap, and never look back. In some unlikely way, Patty had escaped Lorene. Even though she spent most of her afternoons baby-sitting the little ones, Patty was a different breed.

She helped Elizabeth pry Cissie and L'il Joe from the TV with promises of marshmallow in their cocoa and two big stories afterwards. Cissie insisted on three and Elizabeth, eager to get them off to bed, gave in; time was of the essence now. As she read, the vague plans that had begun to form at dinner took on a more concrete shape. The little ones close to sleep, she now had to take care of Patty, who had slipped back to the kitchen and her library book. Patty would be less simple to deal with.

"That must be some book! And you've got a cold! How about snuggling into bed, Patty, and letting me take care of you? I'll bring you some hot lemonade in the best china, and I'll bet Lorene has some cookies hidden. If I can't find them, you can. What about it?"

The eyes narrowed suspiciously for a second. Then, "Can I read in bed?"

"Sure, why not?" She'd take care of that later.

As Elizabeth had rightly guessed, Patty led her straight to the place where Lorene kept a cache of shortbread. Then, while Patty undressed and crawled into bed, Elizabeth used Lorene's best china to prepare a tea tray, with a dainty linen napkin and thinly sliced lemon floating on the hot lemonade. Taking pains with the tea tray when time was so precious might help throw off Patty's suspicions. While Patty sat up in bed, delighted with this unexpected attention, Elizabeth rummaged through the closet, throwing two pairs of almost new jeans on the bed that were followed by a shirt and several jerseys. Out from the back of her closet came the ski clothes she hadn't used for a year. Then she began searching through the drawers of the tiny dresser.

"What are you doing?" Patty asked as she watched.

"I've got to take these things to the cleaners," she explained, hoping Patty wouldn't notice that everything she took out was already quite clean. She came across a slender gold link bracelet that Patty had once admired and gave it to her.

"For you," she said.

"For me? To keep? Oh Liz, I love it. I'll always love it. You really mean it? You're not just fooling?" Her eyes shone as she clasped the bracelet around her wrist. Then a small suspicious, "Why, Elizabeth?"

"Because you've been such a darling, waking me up through my nightmares and all. Please, I do want you to have it."

It wasn't a bribe after all, she thought. She wanted

36

Patty to have the bracelet, and she caught herself in time as she was about to add, "So that you will remember me."

"And now, friend, it's way past your bedtime, so how about some sleep? You don't want big circles under your eyes, do you? And don't worry, I won't tell your mother you stayed up to ten o'clock reading."

Now that really was a bribe, because Lorene, impatient with girls who read too many books, could be mean to Patty. It also implied that she, Elizabeth, would still be around when Lorene came home. Patty threw her arms around Elizabeth and let Elizabeth kiss her on the forehead, tuck the blankets around her, and turn out the light.

"You're nice, Elizabeth," Patty said and fell asleep almost instantly.

"Now, I've got to rush," Elizabeth thought as she gathered up her clothes, some toilet articles from the bathroom, a new towel, and then rushed downstairs. The Himalaya backpack she wore when she hiked through the Sierras with her father and Mark was hanging in the garage; Elizabeth took it down and hurriedly packed her clothes in it. She paused before her father's fishing knife in its slender sheath; would she be wise to take it? She had heard lurid tales about hitch-hikers. All right, she'd take it. It packed easily inside her boot.

"Money, I'll need money," she realized. She had only twelve dollars and a little change. There must be some in the house somewhere. Her father used credit cards and wouldn't have much around. Lorene? Of course. One day she had unexpectedly come on her stepmother kneeling in front of her closet, a shoe box in her hand.

Her last pupil had just left, and Elizabeth wouldn't have thought anything about it, but Lorene had giggled nervously when she saw her. Now instinct told her that's where the money was hidden.

The sight of at least fifteen shoe boxes in Lorene's closet unnerved Elizabeth, but she put her fears aside. No time for fear. And what if she should turn to find Patty standing at the door? Well, she'd have to make something up. If she had to, she could. Good heavens, had Lorene ever thrown away a pair of shoes? Box after box revealed old pumps with heels, from high school, I'll bet, Elizabeth guessed as she went on rapidly to the other boxes. Dull sandals that were heavy without being stylishly clunky, practical shoes for fallen arches, tennis shoes, more tennis shoes, cheap red pumps with rhinestones even. Elizabeth paused and was almost sorry for Lorene; she had such bad taste. And where on earth was the money? She was already taking on the emotions of a thief as she found herself getting angry with Lorene for hiding it so well. Finally, in the last box under a pair of worn bedroom slippers, she found a number of small sealed brown envelopes, a neat "100" penciled on each with a date.

"Lorene, you pack rat! You miser!"

Still, she took only one envelope, checking first to see if there really were a hundred dollars in it. Ten ten-dollar bills! She pushed the other boxes back quickly and put the envelope in her jeans pocket.

To her surprise she felt neither guilt nor fear. She made no promises to herself that she would pay it back, nor did she rationalize that Lorene owed her that much in baby-sitting after all this time, or that if it weren't for Lorene, her father would have given her far more money than that during the last four months. In an instant she understood what it was to be a thief. She needed money and there it was, lying there. It was only common sense for her to take it.

She checked in on the children and found them asleep, looking peaceful and angel-like.

She tiptoed downstairs and went to Mark's room, where she wrote a message.

Dear Mark:
Don't worry about me. You stay until school's out. Okay? I'll see you in Sac. Take care of Dad if you can. It's not easy for him either. I'll miss you.

> Lots of love, bub,
> Liz

She left the note in his school notebook so that most likely he wouldn't find it until the next day. That would give her time to get away. In any event, Mark would know just when to show it to his father. He was an intuitive kid.

She put on her ski jacket, cap, gloves and tried on the knapsack for size. It might be April, but it was still cold. The pack was unbalanced; it was getting late. She re-packed it quickly, and this time it was comfortable enough. Nearly ten-thirty. Mark would be home soon.

She opened the front door, stepped outside, and took a deep breath of cold night air. It calmed her instantly, and she hesitated.

"What is this crazy thing I'm doing?" she asked herself.

Yet she closed the door behind her, listening to the lock click. She broke into a run so that she would catch the bus. In a few minutes she would be at the edge of town where all the hitch-hikers stood when they waited for rides going west.

# II
# Trekking

Elizabeth knew that April, even late April, did not necessarily mean spring, at least not in Nebraska, but she wasn't prepared for the blast of wintry wind that assaulted her as she waited by the side of the road. Lorene's house, always overheated to the point of being stifling, made her even more vulnerable. She shivered, yet the cold sobered her mind.

As she stood alone under the streetlight where she had seen other hitch-hikers stand before, her decision to leave Lincoln began to waver. Not only was it literally a cold world, but she found it difficult to beg for a ride.

Elizabeth wondered if she looked as anonymous to passing motorists as other hikers. The uniform was the same: jeans, boots, sweater and jacket, a long woolen scarf around her neck, and on her head a blue skating cap her mother had once crocheted for her during long waits at rehearsals. Certainly she was visible under the intense light of the streetlamp, yet car after car whizzed by, leaving the air vibrating.

Lorene's house no longer seemed so unendurable. For a few seconds it took on overtones of coziness, and Elizabeth hesitated.

"It's not too late. I could still go back and nobody would know I'd left."

The plan to go back shaped itself as easily as the plan

to leave. If Lorene and her father were home, she could leave the backpack in Mark's room — he had a private entrance — and she could make up a story about having taken a walk to mail a letter. Or she could refuse to discuss it. Yes, after the way they had acted, she would do well to retain a distance until they came to her.

The very thought of the two of them made her angry all over again. Nothing could be done with Lorene because she was impossible, but to think that her own father had acted so weakly! She certainly should leave. If she went back now, it would be another defeat, another loss of face.

Loss of face! The unfortunate expression suddenly reminded her of a story she had read only the week before in the newspaper about a girl hitch-hiker who had been picked up and later found within ten miles of her home; she had been raped and then disfigured for life because her assailant threw acid in her face before leaving her in a ditch.

A flood of long-forgotten stories came to Elizabeth as she stood under the streetlight, her thumb out. Hitch-hikers slashed with knives and left for dead; newspaper photos of a shallow grave by the roadside and a strangled girl; the story of the girl who had been raped while her boyfriend was forced to watch, his being tortured and shot, and then she herself shot but not killed, only paralyzed for life. Another story of a girl picked up by a woman and taken to an apartment where . . .

"I must think of something else," she said, now shivering with fear as well as cold. She forced herself to think of the camellias in Sacramento; would they be blooming? No, they were probably past, but the almond trees

43

might be in bloom or even the cherry tree in the yard. Her father had been so in love with his flowering cherry that he had put a spotlight on it when it bloomed, so that everyone could see it at night, and he would not miss any of its beauty. Some people had criticized him for showing off, but her mother had defended him stoutly. She remembered him putting his arm around her one night as she was going to bed and saying, "Look, Liz, it really is a miracle, isn't it? All that fragrance blooming like that." Remembering this, Elizabeth felt softer toward her father. He could be so tender.

The next day Miss Isham would be waiting for her to come for the appointment she had made. What a shame it would be to miss it! Maybe it would be best to go home after all. Nobody, except Mark perhaps, who would never tell, would be the wiser.

A fat bus was lumbering up to the bus stop across the street. All right, then, she'd go home. Nobody was giving her a ride anyway, and she couldn't take much more of the cold. She was about to hurry across the street to meet the bus when a car pulled up, and a man called to her.

"Want a ride?"

The driver looked respectable, a man about as old as her father, and his voice was friendly without being too familiar. "I'll be driving west for another hour or so. If you want to come along, hop in."

Elizabeth believed in signs, and this was a sign. If her fate or angel or whoever-looked-after-her hadn't wanted her to go, it would have let her reach the bus before this car came by.

"Thank you," she said, her voice surprisingly natural inasmuch as her teeth were chattering with the cold, and she was surprised to find herself frightened. Her heart seemed to have doubled its beat and her stomach

44

fluttered perilously. Yet she began to climb into the car, then remembered she had to take off her backpack first. With an embarrassed titter, she took it off, then sat in the front seat as close to the door as she could get. She smiled shyly at the driver in thanks, then looked straight ahead as the car roared up the ramp and on to the highway.

The fear gave way to exhilaration and as the car picked up speed, she smiled in triumph. This was her decision, her very own decision. She was on her way home *now*!

# 9

He didn't look much like a rapist or murderer, Elizabeth thought, more like a husband and father, a small home, Sunday paper strewn around the living room and a TV blaring out the baseball game, he with a can of beer and a wife making pies in the kitchen. A nice man. But then, how did one know? Instincts told her he was just that, a friendly man giving her a ride. Imagination told her to watch out; in movies it was just this sort of nice man that turned out to be the killer.

"What's a girl like you doing on the highway this time of night?" He had a winning smile and a soft-spoken voice that suggested she could confide in him.

"I'm going home to be with my mother," Elizabeth said. Funny, it was true enough, but it sounded like a lie.

"That's nice. She'll be glad to see you, a pretty girl like you. Where does she live?"

45

She remembered it wasn't wise to give correct names or addresses.

"My mother lives in Denver and my father is in Omaha. They're divorced, and I've been living with my father. But I'd like to be with my mother now."

"Oh sure. I'll bet you miss her like anything. Divorces are sure hard on kids; adults too. All these impossible choices you have to make, like whether to live with your mother or your father. But honey, why didn't your father give you bus fare? All right, don't tell me if you don't want to. It's okay. I'll bet your father don't know you're here, right?"

How did he know that? Well, she didn't have to answer him, although she was beginning to think she could trust him. He went on talking.

"Boy, all the trouble you see today. Divorces, marriages breaking up right and left, and half the kids not bothering to get married. Sometimes you can't blame them. Well, I'm lucky. My wife and me, we get along beautiful. Always have. Trust each other. I don' worry about her and she don' worry about me. Doesn't have to. And I'm on the road selling, so there's all the opportunity a person could want. Nah, I'm old-fashioned. It's best."

Elizabeth thought she was in for an hour of preaching, gentle though it might be. Still, he made sense. If only her mother and father had had the kind of faith he talked about . . . *don't think about it, Elizabeth, it's over.*

"I'll bet you don't know the one thing that really gets us down, the wife and I," he was grinning from ear to ear and Elizabeth decided that probably he wasn't going to preach after all. A story or joke was on the way. "C'mon, guess."

46

"Gee, I don't know, really. Politics?"

"That too, you betcha, but that's not what I'm thinking of. It's a big problem, but not like other big problems. You can't guess it? One word only? All right, I'll tell you. One awful word. *Crabgrass!*"

"Crabgrass?"

"Yeah. You know, that evil green stuff that comes up in your lawn and garden. Nobody invited it; it just comes and takes over. It's gonna take over the world, believe me. All the time I'm driving, I'm thinking, it's takin' over my lawn, is it takin' over my sidewalk, is it walkin' into the house and takin' that over too? Pretty soon it will ask me to move out. So tell me, young lady, if you wanted to have a nice lawn and a good yard and all that crabgrass was coming in, what would you do?"

"He could be a little crazy," she thought, but when she looked at his rounded profile, she changed her mind. He was making conversation, not very good conversation perhaps, but still something to steer her away from the turmoil she still felt. She ought to answer his question. She tried to think about crabgrass but could recall only how her father used to swear about it.

"Personally, I don't worry about crabgrass. I'm sorry."

"Don't be sorry. That kind of worry comes later. But what would you do if?"

"Well, I wouldn't want to spray it because of the ecology thing. Pull it out by hand?"

"Two grow back for every one you pull up."

"Then I'd — um, I'd have a big picnic on it anyway. Just to show it I didn't care."

"Now you're talkin'. Don't get ulcers over crabgrass, right? I'll tell the wife and we'll have us a picnic. Not bad!"

He was chuckling, perhaps more to brighten her up

than because the idea of a picnic on crabgrass was all that funny. He went on to talk about how his wife liked growing roses and how well his boys did in Little League, except Barry, who had problems catching the ball, and asked did Elizabeth make her own clothes. His daughter did just that, very nice too. A good thing for girls to do. Time flew. Elizabeth's head was drooping when the man turned to her unexpectedly.

"What is your name?"

"Elizabeth van Vliet," she said without thinking.

"Mary Lou, did you say? Mary Lou's a nice name." So he told her what she should have remembered. Never give your real name.

At the next intersection he pulled over to the shoulder of the road.

"This is it, Mary Lou. I turn north here, and it's not the right direction for you." He looked at his watch. "Just like I told you, an hour and a half. Now, Mary Lou, tell me the truth. Are you hungry? Did you have dinner tonight?"

"Yes, thanks, I did. Really."

He became serious now, a father talking to a daughter. "All right, I was going to treat you to dinner if you were hungry. Now listen, dear, you are a very nice girl, I can see that, and I don't know what went wrong with you and your papa, but when you get to your mother's, stay put for a while. And don't go wandering around like this again because it can be bad business. You know what I mean; you're a bright girl. So be careful. All right?"

She nodded. "Yes. You are a very nice man. Thanks." After she took out her backpack, she put out her hand and he squeezed it.

48

"Thank *you* for the pleasant company. And remember what I said about staying with your mother. Good luck, Mary Lou!" he called out and drove away.

She was alone again, but pleased that her first encounter had gone well. She was unraped, unassaulted, unrobbed, unbeaten and not even insulted, a sign that the rest of her trip would go well too. Filled with confidence, she believed the trip would not take long and soon she'd be in Sacramento.

Five minutes later a car stopped for her down the road. She hoisted the pack to her shoulders and ran. What good luck!

# 10

"Hi!" she said, feeling friendly now, as she climbed in the car, hardly looking at the driver as she loosened the pack from her shoulders. It was an old car, just how old she couldn't guess, but still it was better than walking.

"Goin' west, are ye?" the driver's voice was curiously flat and drawn out, a farmer's voice, Elizabeth guessed. A tall, unsmiling man. Had he announced he was a "God-fearin' man" she wouldn't have been surprised.

Elizabeth put the backpack on the seat between them, and the Chevy plodded ahead steadily for at least ten minutes without either of them saying anything. Elizabeth wondered if the car had a heater and wished he would turn it on, but a look at the hard-lined profile suggested he liked being chilly and she would do well to like it too.

After ten minutes of cold silence in which she had to convince herself that it was she, Elizabeth, on the road with some back-country farmer, he spoke.

"Where you runnin' off to, Miss?" The flat voice startled her; it had a rusty quality as if the man did not speak very often.

"I'm not 'runnin' off.' I'm going to Denver to be with my mother. She lives there."

"Well, watcha standin' on the highway thumbin' rides for? It's agin' the law. What's the matter with takin' a bus? Does your father know what you're doin', Miss?"

"I'm low on money and it's a long way."

"You're mighty young to be gaddin' about on the highway."

Elizabeth drew her breath in deeply and decided not to answer. Giving her a ride didn't give him the right to grill her. Noting her reticence, he clamped his mouth tight, and for the next half-hour they rode in silence except for an occasional wheezing and clanking from the car. Elizabeth dozed off, and when she woke up, she had no idea how long she had slept.

"Are we still in Nebraska?"

"Yep." It goes on and on and on, she thought; it must stretch at least halfway across the country. She dozed off again until his voice startled her.

"I got a daughter, 'bout your age, I guess. Y'know what I'd do with her if I ever caught her hitchin' a ride with a stranger? 'Course she's got too much sense. Wouldn't do a fool thing like that. . . ."

"Whoop-ti-do! Bully for her!" Elizabeth resisted the urge to say it, even in a low voice. The lecture continued its deliberate way, like a tank going over a hill.

"But naow, if I ever caught her doin' sech a thing, big as she is, a lot bigger'n you, I'd give it to her proper. With my strop. A good stroppin'. That's the way to raise kids. All this permissive behavior, lettin' kids do what they want, and you got kids they ain't worth a nickel. I'd take that strop . . ."

Elizabeth looked at him with horror. Were his eyes really gleaming as though he would love to strop someone, or was it the moonlight that made them shine?

"I brought her up in a good Christian home. Good Christian upbringin'. And I got me a decent good girl. What would yo' paw say if he knew you was out pickin' up rides? I'll bet he don't know, does he?"

"My father is the kind of man who *thinks*," she answered with some indignation, "and if he knew I was on the highway, he'd want to know why; what was wrong with our family that I wanted to leave it. And he would never ever strop me. He loves me. If I did something he didn't like, we would sit down and talk and see what we could do to make things work better."

No sooner had she said this, than she blamed herself for not having kept her mouth shut. It was nonsense, anyway, for, although her father would never touch her, he'd give her a hard time before settling down to a civilized talk. And he would look gloomy and hurt for a long time after. Still, through it all, she would know he loved her.

"Your folks, they're dee-vorced?" the driver asked.

"Yes."

"Women. We spoil 'em. Make 'em think they're somethin' special. You take this women's lib now . . ."

"Let him lecture," she thought, "let him rave." Sooner or later the ride would end. She looked out of the window at the night, deep horizontal shades of blue and deeper blues and purples and inky blacks. The hills were beginning to roll and rise out of the flatness and what seemed to be steeper hills ahead made her realize they really were going west.

"You listenin' to me, young lady?"

"Yes, sir. I'm listenin'." Might as well play along with him.

But as she looked at his stern profile this time, fear prickled along her spine. This was a man with fierce hatreds and endless resentments that had long been bottled up. If she could keep him talking, perhaps everything would work out all right. It was all she could do, she realized, as she saw the situation in a new light; the two of them isolated in this widespread landscape in which not a single house was to be seen and even the highway, except for an occasional truck rumbling by, was empty.

The driver finished talking, and now Elizabeth's fear mounted as he slowed down on the shoulder of the road. She felt for her knife, praying she would not have to use it. Her heart could have broken apart with thumping as the car came to a full stop, and the driver turned off the ignition with a decisive switch of the key. He looked at her directly for the first time, and she was paralyzed with fear by the hard set of the eyes and the tight unsmiling lips.

"Out, girl, get out here," he ordered.

"Here?" her voice squeaked, her throat was so parched. "B-b-but there's nothing here, no houses, no roads, no cars."

"That's right, girl. Jest the way I planned it. Someday you'll thank me for this because I'm gonna teach you a lesson. I'm a good, clean Christian and I won't touch a

52

hair of your head, just teach you a lesson, not to run off and leave your daddy and take up rides with strange men. So, git now, girl, git!"

"Could you, well, do you think you could possibly, if you don't mind, let me off at the next gas station or even a crossroad?"

"Won't larn you nothin' that way. Out here you'll larn good and you won't never forgit. So, git now, 'fore I git mad."

Elizabeth shrank back terrified as he leaned over and opened the car door for her. At least he was careful not to touch her. No choice. She picked up her backpack and stepped out. Once outside, courage returned and she spoke to him.

"Would you really want someone to do *this* to your daughter?"

In answer, he slammed the door and drove off, his tires grating along the gravel as he did so.

She stood there alone.

The wind had died down and the cold night air was still but penetrating. Her teeth chattered, and she shivered uncontrollably. Never before had the world seemed so immense, the sky was so far above, and the dark fields stretched out forever. What was she going to do now?

She stood and shivered, unable to move.

Lights bobbed in the distance. Saved! A car, no, two cars, no, three cars were coming along. She was lucky after all. As they approached she came to life, jumped up and down frantically and waved a white handkerchief, signaling them to stop. She concentrated with as much intensity as she could muster. She cried out, begging the cars to stop. But the drivers either did not

53

see her or didn't care. All three sped past and left her more alone than ever.

Now her eyes brimmed with hot tears. Never before had she been so utterly lost and so completely alone. It was unthinkable that the universe could be so enormous, and she could be so small.

What about God? Was He really there? She had never thought about Him very much. She'd been to church a few times and sung hymns but it had little to do with what had just happened. Again she asked, was He really there? Was anyone there? Did He or anyone know that she was standing there alone and abandoned under the great sky in the middle of this dark, still landscape without even the distant light of a farmhouse to show that someone, anyone at all, beside herself, existed?

She whimpered as though she were a child of six, oblivious to the tears that streamed down her cheeks. The Kleenex she used to dab at her face was sodden. After a while — she did not know how long — the weeping spasm stopped, and she came to her senses. Standing there could mean getting a bad cold, but if she walked, eventually she'd find a house, a gas station or some sign of human habitation.

Walking drove some of the fear away. Doing something, moving, taking action, anything like that was better than aimless waiting. She must remember this, write it down somewhere, tell Miss Isham about it sometime. Miss Isham would be pleased that she had discovered this.

Courage, that's what she needed. All right, then, courage.

Once she remembered she'd been even colder than

she was now, but snow coldness was different from this. That time the four of them — she, Rick, Ken and Linda — had been skiing; the snow had begun to fall heavily in thick flakes, so they had just one more run and then stopped off at the round ski hut at Squaw Valley. The sudden warmth was almost overwhelming after the cold. They had sat at a wooden table, their hands curled around mugs of steaming chocolate, while outside the snowflakes drifted this way and that.

A group of seven or eight young men sat at another table and she had watched them, impressed because they were all so good-looking and vigorous and joked so easily in a language she didn't understand. Her friends had argued about their nationality. She thought that they were Scandinavian; Linda and Ken said no, they must be Austrian or Swiss; Rick had said he couldn't care less. The arguing stopped when one of the young men picked up an accordion and played while the others joined in.

So beautiful! The bright young men and the singing and the snowflakes falling outside, she wanted to treasure them forever, trap them inside a glass ball where it would snow forever. There was one of the young men in particular, the darkest of the group with thick hair and serious brown eyes which, once they found Elizabeth, never left her. She had returned the look, taking in the ruddy cheeks and full lips, the very knit of his heavy skiing sweater. Embarrassed at being caught staring, she had lowered her glance but looked up again and found him still watching her. The accordionist took up another tune, this time more raucous and with words that were probably off-color since the young men singing had poked each other as they sang. Still the young man with the dark eyes looked at Elizabeth, and she looked back. Without a single word, they were together, as though nobody else in the world existed.

"I love him." She had said the words to herself then and it was as true and factual as saying that he had brown eyes or that his hair was wavy.

Rick had noticed the young man's glances and had become jealous. He insisted loudly that they start for home right then without waiting another minute, or the highway would be impassable. So they had left.

Now, two years later, as she walked along the highway, it seemed odd that she could remember the young man at the ski lodge so well, practically in photographic detail, as though she had just seen him, whereas Rick was still a blur.

"But, of course, it will be different once I see him," she consoled herself. Again she conjured a scene with him, driving down Highway 101 with the hot sun above, the refreshing salt breezes off the Pacific and Rick's arm around her.

A lone cry, a shriek from a bird or an animal stabbed the midnight air in some unknown anguish and immediately she was alone again, more frightened than before.

"Help me! Help me!" she cried out loud, but her voice died in the black night air. "I'm so scared. Please help me!" she wailed.

Maybe someone would hear. God. Or her luck would change. She would never know, but as she walked to the crest of the hill she saw in the distance the dark towers of two grain elevators, the castles of Nebraska, and she was grateful. A few steps farther on she saw over the hill the most welcome sight in all the world, a blazing red neon sign vibrating GAS and EATS. She had to squint to read it, since her glasses were packed away. The *A*'s in the sign kept blinking out, but no matter. It was a shelter. Someone must be there, and that was exactly where she was going to go.

She hurried on, almost running. Once more she dared to hope. Everything was going to be all right.

# 11

Trucks large and small waited outside GAS and EATS like ghostly mastodons in the moonlight. As Elizabeth came closer to the lunchroom, she could hear sounds from a jukebox assaulting the night; yet harsh as the music was, Elizabeth felt relief in hearing it. She wasn't the last living creature on earth after all!

Bursts of male laughter mingled with the music, and she hesitated before opening the door and slipping in. The diner, a long warm room vibrating in clouds of steam and cigar smoke, was filled with men, some sitting at tables and others on stools at the long counter. The loud easy talking stopped as the message that a girl had entered silently circulated through the room. Every head in the place turned toward Elizabeth, who hesitated at the door, her hand still on the handle as though she might run back into the night. She felt exposed, as though a giant spotlight were focused on her, but the men soon turned back to their dinners, and the talking began again — although this time it was more quiet.

Were there no women here at all? One, a waitress

leaning over a table in the far corner. From the subdued tone of the talking and sudden burst of laughter, Elizabeth supposed they were telling jokes, probably off-color ones at that. Her hand tightened on the doorknob.

"It's all right, dear. You can come in. I won't let the wild beasts hurt you." It was the man at the counter who spoke to her.

A quick red blushed her cheeks as a snicker passed down the length of the counter. Two men turned to look at her again, and she thought they were licking their lips. Over her or their pork chops? She was so tired, she no longer knew what she actually saw or what she imagined.

"Really, it's all right. You can sit here, if you like," the counterman said. Taking off her backpack, she sat at the counter near the wall.

"What can I get for you, Miss?" the counterman asked, while his eyes told her not to worry; nobody would hurt her.

"Coffee and buttered toast, please," she whispered, although she would have preferred hot chocolate like the kind she had made for Lorene's children. Was it only four hours ago? Already Lincoln had slipped into an experience long past.

The coffee was hot, and she sipped it slowly, hoping to make it last. Although now and then she was aware of a man looking at her, she kept her eyes lowered and wondered with a new sense of worry where she would spend the night. Even if there were a motel or hotel nearby, there'd be problems about registering. It was not at all unlikely that by this time her father had notified the police, and they would be looking for her. They might even be looking for her in a diner like this. Never before had she known the fear of being hunted.

"More coffee? Won't cost you nothin' after the first cup," the counterman said as he filled her cup again. "How about a piece of pie?"

"No. Thanks all the same."

One of the drivers at the counter called out, "Hey, Al, give her a piece of apple pie. Unless she'd rather have cherry. Or mince? Anything, the treat's on me."

Elizabeth looked up. "That's nice of you, but I couldn't really. I'm not very hungry."

"Okay, sis," he said. But it was the man next to him, a stocky man with a balding head and direct blue eyes, who walked over to Elizabeth.

"If you're looking for a ride, I can take you as far as Lincoln."

To *Lincoln*? She stifled a desire to laugh at this twist of events. Was it a sign? For a moment she was tempted to go back with him. This driver impressed her as being straight and she had no fears of him; going back meant avoiding all the problems she was continually meeting.

But the van Vliet stubbornness was stronger in her than she had expected. She was much like her father, after all. If she set out for Sacramento, then she'd go to Sacramento, and that was all there was to it.

"Thanks very much, but I'm headed west," she smiled at the driver.

"Okay, sister." He waved goodbye to Al, wished Elizabeth good luck, and went out into the night.

Now what to do? She looked into her empty cup as though it held the answer. She couldn't stay there all night, yet every time someone opened the door and she felt the chill of the night, she shivered at the thought of going back out again.

Two figures came in. A chorus of "Hey, Johnnie!" arose from a table at the rear, and Johnnie went over to join them while the slighter, younger newcomer looked around the room, and, seeing Elizabeth, went over to sit at the empty stool beside her.

Elizabeth was grateful when she saw that the figure was a girl. She removed her large well-filled backpack and laid it beside Elizabeth's. The easy smile, the wide Slavic face and bright dark eyes reassured her, as if this girl were saying, everything's fine, don't worry. As she sat down, she took off her cap, an unusual combination of bone-white knitted yarn with narrow strips of white leather woven in. When she shook her head, a mass of thick black hair tumbled down.

"Hi," she said to Elizabeth. "It's some night out there. Brrrrr!" Before Elizabeth could say anything, the counterman came over and without hesitating, the girl ordered a bowl of hot chili.

"How about you? You want some too? Best thing for a cold night. Coffee's warm but it doesn't stay with you."

Elizabeth shook her head. "Everybody's trying to feed me. I'm not really hungry. Thanks anyway."

"Sure. That your backpack? Where are you going?"

"Sacramento. And you?"

"Hey, what about that! San Francisco. We can go together, if you like."

A relief such as Elizabeth had never known flooded through her veins, and she could practically feel the tenseness in her muscles quieting. Her voice quavered as she spoke. "That would be marvelous."

The counterman placed a bowl of steaming hot chili in front of the girl, and she ate silently for a few minutes, concentrating on her food as though she were really hungry. Then she put down her spoon and turned to Elizabeth.

60

"Something bad happened to you, didn't it? Something recent. I can feel it in you. You're still quivering. Want to tell me?"

"It wasn't anything much. It's over now anyway."

"I'll listen if you want to talk about it. Better to get it out of your system than have it stay there and rot," the girl said, taking another spoonful of chili. Elizabeth found that she did want to tell her about it.

"This man, some kind of farmer, I think, picked me up and sort of lectured to me for about half an hour. Then he stopped the car and made me get out, about four miles back. He was a little crazy, I think. Said he wanted to teach me a lesson. He didn't touch me, so I guess it could have been worse. But he really frightened me. That's all."

"That's all? That's enough, the bastard. But at least you did get out all right. You look so young. And you're right, it could have been lots worse. With two of us traveling together, we won't be taking such chances. How long have you been on the road?"

"Since about ten o'clock tonight."

"I guess this is something new for you, isn't it? Well, after awhile you'll begin to have feelings about drivers, and you'll avoid the nuts and freaks. We may as well get acquainted; I'm Maija Hrdlka."

At Elizabeth's puzzled expression, she smiled as though she knew her name was something of a hurdle. She pronounced it slowly. "My-a Herd-lick-a. Czech. And you?"

"Elizabeth van Vliet."

"That's your real name? It fits you; it really does. Something aristocratic about it."

Elizabeth found herself blushing. She had often been

accused of putting on airs and the "van" in her name only set her apart even more.

"It really is my name, for better or worse. Yours is pretty unusual, Maija."

"It bothers people. When they have to spell it, it's traumatic!" she laughed, going back to her chili.

Elizabeth wondered if she really came from Czechoslovakia. A slight accent suggested that she could be foreign, but it also sounded like the speech of certain Americans she'd heard, mostly on TV programs. An eastern accent, was that it?

"See those drivers?" Maija said, "I think they're getting ready to leave soon — they're on their second cup of coffee — and maybe I can find out about a ride for us. If you want to go to the Ladies' and get washed, I'll join you there in a few minutes."

"All right," Elizabeth said, amazed at how docile she was. "I could have managed on my own, one way or another," she told herself, but she was surprised at how willing she was to let Maija take over. In the washroom she took out her soap and washcloth and was scrubbing her face when Maija came in.

"Great luck for us! A ride to the next town, but we'll have to hurry. What did you plan to do about sleeping tonight?"

"I hadn't really thought about it. I left home rather unexpectedly."

"I guess so."

Maija laughed. Quickly she brushed her teeth, using baking soda from a yellow box, and scrubbed her face until it shone. She wrapped up her toilet articles and was ready to go while Elizabeth was still brushing her hair.

"I could use a nice long hot bath," Elizabeth mused and Maija answered briskly, "I'll arrange it the next time, Madam," grinning broadly so that Elizabeth had to smile at the ridiculousness of it.

Then she picked up her backpack and followed Maija outside into the night.

# 12

It was Elizabeth's first experience in a truck, and she was surprised to find how high they sat, how the cab seemed like a little room, and how much power there was in the great beast. Ahead the gray road stretched converging into lines like a lesson in perspective. The sky was an upside-down bowl perforated with stars, an unevenly punctured collander. With a new friend beside her, everything would be all right. Now she felt an exhilaration as the miles passed beneath them. Maybe it was how a snake felt when he shed his old skin to find himself new and ready to begin once more.

Maija's hand found hers and squeezed it gently. She was no longer alone in the world.

Half an hour later they came to a small town, and Maija asked the driver to let them off at the stoplight. After the warmth of the cab, the blowing of wind that greeted the girls shocked Elizabeth into wakefulness.

"There's probably a church nearby and a churchyard. Ever sleep in one?"

"No. Have you?" Elizabeth asked doubtfully.

"It works out very well. Nobody bothers you much. I hope you have a sleeping bag."

"I'm sorry, Maija. I packed in such a hurry, I didn't think about it."

"Never mind. We can both wiggle into mine. I guess this must be it."

The gate to the graveyard that rested beside the church was locked, but even with her backpack, Maija climbed over the fence easily and turned to help Elizabeth, who felt doubtful about doing such a thing. Wasn't it sacrilegious?

"You're sure it's all right to sleep here?"

"Why not? We aren't going to hurt anyone. I don't think we'll disturb the natives. And this is a good one. Look at those Italian cypresses there, such marvelous trees, and soft grass and sculptures. Just think, Elizabeth, so many people never enjoy such things as trees and sculpture when they are living. They have to wait until they die to get surrounded with this loveliness."

In almost no time at all, Maija found a good place, unfastened the sleeping bag which had swung from the bottom of her pack, and laid it out. She put her shoes in the pack so they'd be dry in the morning and Elizabeth copied her, being careful not to ask too many questions. Once the sleeping bag was laid out, Maija bowed.

"Be my guest!"

"I couldn't really. It looks so small. I'd crowd you too much."

"We'll manage. Go ahead, Elizabeth, get in."

Elizabeth crawled in, embarrassed by this unforeseen dilemma. It would be uncomfortable to face her new friend, and yet it would be rude to turn her back on her. Was there such a thing as sleeping-bag etiquette?

Such matters didn't faze Maija, who crawled in rapidly after Elizabeth, took care of her awkwardness by embracing her quickly, and then turned around so that Elizabeth could curl up snugly against the strong back. This would have settled it, but Elizabeth decided she ought to warn Maija about the dreams.

"Maija, I think I'd better tell you something. I have nightmares."

"Don't worry about it. I'll wake you if you do."

Elizabeth murmured thanks, took warmth from Maija, and in the next breath fell sound asleep. Maija slept too, but later, turning in her sleep, awoke; she studied the pale oval face and long wisps of silken hair that fell around it, then fell asleep again.

# 13

The morning sun beamed into Elizabeth's face and she woke, puzzled at first, but then remembering where she was. She stretched, yawned, and had a gratifying sense of well-being. No nightmares! She turned to look at Maija, but there was no sign of her.

Sitting up, she turned around and discovered her friend sitting erect on the ground in front of a sturdy tree. A rope was tied around her waist at one end and attached to a kind of loom that was fastened around the trunk of the tree at the other end. She was intent on knotting or weaving something, her fingers working as fast and accurately as the fingers of a concert pianist.

She turned to Elizabeth, not pausing for an instant in her rapid weaving.

"Good morning. Did you sleep all right, Elizabeth?"

"It was beautiful. I hope I didn't drive you out."

"Not at all. I get up early. How were the nightmares?"

"Not one. You have no idea what a relief it is. I haven't slept so well in a long time. I'm grateful."

"Why be grateful to me? I didn't have anything to do with it. But I'm glad it worked out that way."

Only, Elizabeth was sure Maija's presence had had something to do with it. The morning sun warmed Elizabeth as she sat up in the sleeping bag, and she knew then that the nightmares would not come back.

Her hair was tousled and she reached for her brush. She would have like to ask Maija what she was doing, but the silence seemed more fitting. She watched Maija's fingers flying back and forth as though they had a skill and intelligence of their own, and she found herself wishing she could do it too. She had such useless hands, untrained for anything.

In the clear morning light, Elizabeth could see that Maija's hair was raven black and her eyes, too, were a deep color, a very dark blue. Guessing her age was another matter. When she laughed, a surprisingly hearty laugh, she seemed only fifteen or sixteen, but at other times she might have been as old as twenty-two or twenty-three. Elizabeth guessed twenty-two.

"I'd like to talk to her. She'd be polite, I think, but it would be like talking to someone in the middle of their prayers," Elizabeth thought.

The sun lit the drops of dew on the grass and made patterns on the tombstones, warm and light on the eastern side, damp and cold on the western edge. The

66

light moved slowly, almost imperceptibly as the sun rose. "Good heavens, what am I doing here; is this real?" Elizabeth asked herself. How incredible to find herself sitting somewhere in a graveyard in western Nebraska, and not ten feet away was a girl she had met in a truck-stop the night before, a girl with a peculiar name who was at sunrise sitting tied to a tree, weaving, and apparently meditating.

A bird perched on a gravestone in front of Elizabeth, cocked his eye, and regarded her seriously. "Hello," she said to him. He flew directly up into the sky. "I'm almost as free as you," she thought. Lightness surged through her. She felt a little damp, a little stiff, but good. Amazingly good. And hungry.

At last Maija unfastened the rope from the tree and held out a length of intricate weaving, still unfinished. It reminded Elizabeth of the macrame some of her class-mates used to do, carrying it with them everywhere. Only Maija's weaving was so much more varied and subtle that the comparison wasn't really a good one.

"What's it going to be, Maija?"

"A belt, perhaps," she said, putting it around her waist, "or possibly an ornamental piece for a formal dress. Can you imagine it over velvet, like this . . ." She held the woven piece, incongruous in all its elegance, against her jeans, but the single gesture let Elizabeth imagine exactly what it would be like.

"Or it could be a wall hanging. Or a whatever."

"A what?"

"A whatever is whatever will pay the rent. In other words, these things sell. Are you hungry, Liz? I'm starving. Let's go get breakfast somewhere."

Elizabeth rolled the sleeping bag swiftly. It was

perhaps the only skill she had. She would have liked to be able to tell Maija how impressed she was with her, but she was too awkward to know how to put it, so she said nothing.

The girls hoisted their packs and walked down the main street, a short block with a gas station at either end. Maija laughed at the only restaurant, a fly-specked lunchroom with the ambitious name, *Café de Paris*. The waitress looked at the girls suspiciously as they went into the tiny Ladies' to get washed and brush their hair. Then freshened and combed, they sat opposite each other at a table.

"It's nice having breakfast with someone," Maija said.

Elizabeth smiled. "I was thinking the same thing."

As they waited for the waitress, Elizabeth looked at her new friend and noticed how the side of her face toward the window was light and the other side was in shadow with the black hair a frame around it. She was unaccountably seeing everything in patterns of light and dark, first the gravestones and now this. It was Maija who spoke.

"You're so northern. A northern maiden for sure. Pale. Straight. But not an ice-maiden. I suppose you'll get all honey brown once you hit California again. But I like your paleness, as if you had a pale northern sun in back of you."

"That's a nice thing to say. Thank you," she said, her glance falling in a pleased confusion. So many people talked about the way she looked, always asking why didn't she model or why didn't she go on the stage. What Maija just said pleased her more than any compliment she had ever had, as though she were being seen with different eyes.

68

Maija was about to say something more, when the waitress came over with a pad and a chilly, "Yes, what will you have?"

Elizabeth had eaten in many restaurants, and yet she was always a bit greedy when faced with a menu, even a greasy one such as the one the waitress handed her. She could have ordered everything on it but settled for juice, eggs, bacon, chocolate and waffles — no not waffles after all — but toast. And jam.

"You're going to eat all that, little you?" Maija asked, and for herself ordered boiled eggs and tea.

Now Elizabeth felt guilty. Maybe Maija was broke. She promised to share her breakfast with her and then had a moment of panic while she searched for her wallet, but remembered in time that it wasn't in her jeans pocket but in the pack.

Maija put away in her pocket the two lumps of sugar the waitress brought her for her tea, then asked for more. The waitress brought them with some resentment, slamming them down on the table.

Unruffled, Maija said, "Sometimes when you're hiking and you get worn out, sugar cubes give you energy. Here, take these."

Hiking? What kind of hiking were they going to be doing. Or was Maija expecting long waits between rides?

The girls ate slowly. Four men, walking into the café and sitting at the counter for breakfast, stared at the girls. After all, they were strangers. Elizabeth, catching herself staring at Maija, wondered again what she was doing here, even temporarily coupled with this unusual girl. What a story all this would make when she got back to Sacramento, to Rick and the others! They might not believe it, but it would fascinate them. Yet as Maija winked at her, as if they were having a great time making the waitress wonder who they could be, Elizabeth felt deceitful. She felt as if she had just betrayed this girl who was already a good friend.

Suddenly Elizabeth's fork stopped in mid air as she looked past Maija to see a policeman walking slowly past the café. In panic she thought maybe he was a state trooper who'd been advised to pick up a runaway. Quite likely her father had given a photograph of her to the police. Her hair would be the first giveaway!

"I'll be back in a minute," she whispered to Maija. "Help yourself to the eggs and toast. Please. I'm not hungry anymore." She rushed off to the Ladies' where she tied her hair on top of her head as well as she could, using a handkerchief to hold it together; her skating cap covered it well. Later she would buy hairclips. How else to change her appearance? Glasses. Lorene had urged her to buy the metal-rimmed glasses she did not actually need, and she pulled them out from her pack. Yes, they changed her appearance considerably, she thought, giving her an air of innocence.

"You're sure you're Elizabeth? It's a good change," Maija said, having seen the policeman and having had enough good sense not to ask any questions while they were still in the café. "Let's not rush. There's plenty of time," she warned. And Elizabeth understood.

After they paid their checks and left, the morning took on an air of normal everyday living, as though everything was all right with the world. They walked through the few residential streets of the town, passing three children on their way to school and an old lady with frizzled hair who was sweeping her sidewalk. Only

70

a hound, a good watchdog at the end of a chain, strained forward to bark at them ferociously. Elizabeth thought him capable of murder, but Maija went over to him directly, talked to him soothingly, petted and charmed him. Barking gave way to covering her with kisses and his tail wagged incessantly. If he could, he would have followed them all the way home.

"How did you do that?" Elizabeth asked as the girls walked to the highway.

"Secret methods! Maybe I'll make you my protégée and teach you."

She spoke jokingly, yet she looked seriously at Elizabeth.

"How long will it take us to get out of Nebraska?" Elizabeth asked.

"Forever. What are you running away from?"

While they waited for a car to pick them up, Elizabeth told her what had happened — about the divorce, her father's remarriage, living in Lorene's house, the nightmares, everything.

"And you really did decide on the spur of the moment, just like that? You listened to yourself then? That's great, Liz. There's hope for you!"

Hope for her? Because she decided to leave on the spur of the moment? Almost everyone she knew would have thought it a stupid thing to do, yet here was Maija practically congratulating her for it.

At any rate, there was no time to go deeper into the subject, because a car slowed down for them, and they rushed to get in. The driver, a black-haired young priest with rimless glasses, invited the girls in a strong Spanish accent to ride with him as far as Cheyenne.

Maija stepped in first and Elizabeth sat beside her,

content to let Maija take care of the conversation while she gazed at the landscape of hills that swelled into mountains as they moved west, away from Nebraska.

# 14

There were questions Elizabeth wanted answered, and yet she did not dare to ask. Who are you really, Maija? Where do you come from? What makes you so different from everybody else and what do you really *do*?

Had Elizabeth asked these questions, she knew that Maija would have looked at her, perhaps raising her eyebrows the tiniest bit, and explained simply; or, she might have laughed, or done nothing at all. Her answers might be clear on the surface but filled with secret meanings. They had slept together in a narrow sleeping bag and had trusted each other as they traveled, yet such questions were entirely too personal.

But time on the road was not at all like time in the city, where one had to be in school at a certain hour and home at another. Here, where the land and sky opened wide, promising to roll on forever and ever, there would be time enough for everything. The answers would come of themselves, without her having to ask anything at all.

The noise of the car made it difficult for Elizabeth to hear the conversation between Maija and the priest. She did gather some phrases, and learned that the young priest had come from Madrid originally and was now working with Indians in the area. What more he had to say was blotted out by three aggressive trucks thundering by. The priest shrugged his shoulders; the poor car did as well as she could. When Elizabeth listened again, the priest and Maija had become involved in a philosophical discussion, sparring with one another and apparently enjoying it. Elizabeth, not understanding what they were talking about, looked out of the window and thought about her own problems.

Less than twelve hours before, she had been in Lorene's dining room, clearing the table. And here, after a night of unbelievable adventure, she was riding with a Spanish priest and a decidedly unusual girl, and was quite possibly being sought by the police. In back of her was Lincoln — and, most likely, a frightened, angry father — and in front of her, Sacramento. She'd have to think up a story more believable than the truth for her mother.

"Yet why does it all seem so unimportant now?" she asked herself. Being suspended between Lincoln and Sacramento, sitting beside Maija and watching the landscape unfold, her problems, try as she might to concentrate on them, kept vanishing.

"So you're going to San Francisco," the priest was saying to Maija. "And what will you do when you get there? Do you have friends? A job?"

"A few friends," Maija answered. "I lived there once for a short while. And maybe a job. There's one waiting for me, almost definite, yet not quite."

"What kind of work do you do?"

"I'm a weaver. Specifically, I make tapestries."

He looked at her then. His eyebrows lifted. "Tapestries, did you say?"

"Sure. How about that?" Maija was grinning, apparently having received similar reactions of surprise at this unexpected answer. "The particular job I might get will be a commission for an enormous tapestry which will hang in an important government building. I was recommended as one of the workers. There aren't too many of these jobs around, so keep your fingers crossed for me, will you?"

"Isn't it chancy, going all the way out there when it's not actually settled that you will have a job? What will you do if it falls through?"

"Faith, Father. Something will turn up."

"Faith? Yes, good for you! I think something will turn up; I can feel the faith in you. But tell me, how did you get started in all this tapestry? I didn't think anyone did tapestry after the sixteenth or seventeenth century? Isn't it rather rare these days?"

"Do you really want to know how I got started, Father?"

"I wouldn't have asked. It's an unusual occupation, isn't it? Rather exotic in a way. Where did you learn it?"

"In exotic Hackensack, New Jersey!" Maija laughed. If she came from New Jersey, Elizabeth wondered, perhaps that explained the inflections she used.

"To be as brief as possible, I was going to a city college, working nights, majoring in philosophy and getting more and more unhappy about the way words and ideas kept playing around. I was getting impatient. The words were becoming a burden. Do you understand what I mean, how I felt about it?"

The priest nodded. "Words can become so abstract they simply fade away."

"Exactly. It was getting more and more frustrating. I couldn't get my hands on the words, you see. One day a friend of mine wanted to get some of his drawings from the art department, and while he was talking with his professor, I wandered into the weaving room, where they kept the looms. There were maybe eight looms all strung up and looking impossibly complicated, but there was a young man working there, and as I watched him, it seemed wonderful that he could take all those long slender lengths of fiber and yarn and put them together to make a solid flat piece in complicated patterns.

"Someone had begun a non-loom weaving, hanging from a beam, and I reached out to touch some of the yarns — I believe they were hand spun — that hung down and seemed to be waiting to be touched. As I recall, they were not quite white, probably a natural color, and the spinning had left them a little uneven, fuzzy in some places, but somehow full of life. So I reached out and held them in my fingers. I stood there, with the yarn in my fingers, and then I had a . . . well, a sudden enlightenment, a *satori*. Do you know what I mean?"

The priest nodded. Both he and Elizabeth waited, so Maija went on.

"I felt that these were threads leading to heaven. Not a literal heaven, of course, but a peace, a way of being in balance. They were only thin threads, but I felt if I could learn to use them, to bind and understand them, then I would never have to bother with the *words* of philosophy again. The words would fall away, and I'd be free. All that night I stayed awake wondering if it could be true, or if I were just grasping at anything. When I woke up that next morning, I knew it was true. So I changed all my courses.

"You know what surprised me most? Not that I could

change everything over night, but that my mother could be so upset, even though I was paying my own way and could do what I liked. We were a large family with lots of worries and no money, and I didn't think she'd even notice. But she explained it to me: she said, "I came here from Czechoslovakia to get away from these peasant things, this weaving, this drudgery, and here you are throwing away all your opportunities and going back to the loom. Just think, you could be a teacher!"

"To her that was the height of everything, to be a teacher. But knowing that my ancestors had woven helped me. When I began the handweaving, making the threads go in and out, it felt right, as though I were touching some kind of wisdom my ancestors had. Something that got lost over here."

"You didn't learn all about tapestry in Hackensack, did you?"

"Heavens, no. I had so much to learn. Still do. I went to Norway. I worked in France for almost a year with some weavers at Aubusson, which is where some of the best tapestry is done. Then I met someone from Edinburgh, so I worked in a workshop there, and now I'm hoping that good things will be happening in San Francisco. Enough! I talk *too much*! So I'm going to keep quiet now."

"It's a beautiful story," the priest said. "Thank you for telling me. Grace can come in many ways. I think you must know that." Then he turned to Elizabeth, who had been hanging on Maija's every word. "And are you a weaver too?"

"Who, me? No. I just go to high school."

She shrank back in the seat, feeling ashamed of herself. What did she do? Nothing. Go to high school like millions of others. Follow like a sheep.

76

"And are you going to San Francisco too?" the priest asked, interested and not in the least suggesting there was anything unusual about a high school girl hitch-hiking at that time of year.

"I'm going to Sacramento to be with my mother," she said. If all the priests were like this one, she thought, she would like being a Catholic.

The priest left them off in Cheyenne late that afternoon. He wished them good luck and they thanked him, wishing him the same.

"Cheyenne!" Maija said. "I've always wanted to see it. It looked better in the westerns than it does from here. Want to walk around?"

"I want to do anything you want to do."

Elizabeth was still deeply impressed by what Maija had told the priest. She wasn't quite sure what a tapestry was, remembering only large faded dusty things hanging on the walls in museums, but since Maija was intrigued with Cheyenne at the moment, Elizabeth decided to ask her about tapestries later.

The girls stopped to look in the window of a western clothing store. Fine leather boots, saddles, spurs, belts, western shirts and riding clothes. Some Indian jewelry with turquoise pieces in silver settings.

"Just look at all that! Would you mind going in with me for just a minute?"

"I'd love to."

It was odd, Maija not being one who seemed to care about such things, that she exclaimed over a well-cut jacket and a creamy silk shirt, fluttering her eyes as she looked at the price. "Brrrrrr," she said and put it down.

While Maija admired the boots, Elizabeth picked up the shirt, hoping it was the right size, found a red silk kerchief, gave it to a clerk, and paid for it with bills

77

from Lorene's brown envelope. As they left the store, she gave the bag to Maija.

"What's this?" Maija asked, looking inside.

"A souvenir of our trip. For you."

Maija became serious, almost stern. "Elizabeth, did you steal this?"

"What do you think I am, Maija? I bought it, really — I wanted you to have it."

"You mean, you *bought* this beautiful, terribly, ridiculously expensive shirt for me? And this scarf too?"

She was delighted as a schoolgirl, threw her arms around Elizabeth and kissed her.

"I don't know what to say. Is thank you enough? No, it isn't. But I thank you. I don't need a souvenir because I could never forget you. And I'll always treasure this, for itself, and because it's from you."

Elizabeth blushed, elated that she had done what she had done and that Maija, with her inborn sense of how to behave, had accepted her gifts with grace.

The girls walked through the streets of Cheyenne together. And soon it was time for a bowl of chili.

# 15

After dinner the girls found a ride to Laramie with an older woman who might have come straight out of a TV western. The Brillo-like hair, the leathery skin, the well-worn riding clothes, and the genuine western twang were so perfectly in character that Maija exchanged a brief glance with Elizabeth, both of them wondering if the woman were for real. Maija took up conversation with her with the same ease and grace she had shown in the two previous rides. Soon they discovered that the woman was born and bred in Wyoming and managed a sizeable ranch. "Women can do anything, anything at all," Maija remarked to Elizabeth later on when they talked about her.

Elizabeth was astounded and relieved at the good luck they were having in their drivers, but a sense of uneasiness warned her they would pay for it later. One had to deserve good fortune, and they hadn't earned it yet. "It's my father in me," Elizabeth said. "I never knew before this that I was a puritan, but I guess I am. Everything has to be paid for; nothing is free."

Maija laughed at Elizabeth's fears. "Who says so? Do you think life is all balanced up like a bookkeeping machine?"

The skies were deepening, and dark blue and purple washes warned of night coming on. Shortly after they passed through Laramie, the driver explained she had to turn south, so the girls thanked her for the ride and found themselves at the edge of the road once more. Maija looked around, frowning a little.

"Why does this place look so familiar to me?" She tapped her forehead and then remembered. "Of course, Liz, I've been here before. Right here. It's the beginning of the Medicine Bow Range. I know a place where we can stay, but we'll have to walk a few miles. What do you think?"

"Let's do it. I've been up in the Sierras but never in these mountains."

The girls spoke little as they walked along the road.

The mountain air, higher, thinner and more pure than that Elizabeth was used to, and Maija's rapid, steady pace, used up all her energy.

"We're really going uphill, you know," Maija explained.

After several miles they came to a plateau, wide, flat, high and grassy — about seven thousand feet high. Never had the world seemed so wide nor the sky so high. The cobalt blue deepened into purples so dense that the colors soon became indistinguishable in the night. The stars, hard pinpoint diamonds, twinkled more intensely than Elizabeth had ever seen, and she found herself getting exhilarated and heady, the way she did when she'd had a glass of wine on an empty stomach.

She was relieved when Maija said, "We might as well turn in now. The road runs on like this for a long way. What about this nice wide shoulder here?"

The shoulder was indeed generous, about as wide as the road itself, and Maija explained that the width was needed for driving cattle.

In almost no time at all, the girls unrolled the sleeping bag, brushed out their hair, letting it tumble over their jackets, and shivering all the while, took off their boots. Maija insisted that Elizabeth get in first while she piled their jackets over the sleeping bag. Soon the girls lay comfortably together, warming each other. Elizabeth had never seen the stars so bright.

"Look! There's Cassiopeia's Chair over there. See it?" Elizabeth asked.

"Where? Where? What? Which one is that?"

"Those five bright stars that make a "W" or an "M" over there. And the Big Dipper there, and the Little

Dipper there and, of course, the North Star. I've never seen it so brilliant."

"Where did you learn all this about the stars?" Maija asked, surprised.

"My father. He used to take my brother and me out to an open field or to the park where we'd lie down and watch. My father knows so much about so many things, stars, music, math . . ." Elizabeth hadn't remembered about the stars for a long time, and now a great longing for her father welled up inside of her; he had held her securely once when they were in the Sierras looking up at the stars, and she had almost fainted trying to imagine what a light year really was.

"That's nice, to have your father teach you things. My father was never there and what my poor mom told me didn't have anything to do with stars. Anyway, tell me now, because I am very ignorant about all this. Which one is the Big Dipper and where is the North Star? That would be a good name for a tapestry. Hmm. So let me in on it."

"Everybody knows that, Maija. You're not putting me on, are you?"

"Liz, my little one, in Hackensack when you look up you don't see stars. You see neon signs and streetlights or the wash on someone's line where they forgot to take it in. You have to do so much vertical detouring to find one single star, you forget they exist."

"I'm sorry. Maybe you can make up for it, if you want to."

Elizabeth explained what she remembered, wishing she knew more. She warned Maija that if you looked directly above you could have a frightening sensation of being drawn upward into the sky or an opposite but

81

equally scary sensation of sinking straight down into the center of the earth. "At least it was that way with me," Elizabeth explained. "It still is."

"I've never had that kind of experience before. Let's see." Maija looked straight up, but nothing Elizabeth described happened.

"Maybe it doesn't happen to everyone. Oh, Maija, I'm tired and I hate being chilled, and yet I'm perfectly content. I can hardly believe it."

"Here's something to make your contentment more than perfect. Look at this!" Maija reached into her knapsack and pulled out two chocolate bars.

"I know. It's sinful and idiotic. Chocolate is fattening and does things to your complexion. And we've just brushed our teeth. It makes it all the better, right? *Toujours gai!* But don't get it on the sleeping bag."

"I won't. I love chocolate too."

She wondered why Maija worried about gaining weight when she was actually thin. They lay under the stars and munched chocolate. No more worries about anything.

"Did you really mean what you told the priest, Maija, about holding those strings or fiber or yarns, whatever it was, and feeling the way to heaven? I can't say it the way you did. It was beautiful. You know what I mean."

"Sure, I meant it. It's what I do, what I am. Why?"

"Nothing. I was just thinking about it. Well, nothing like that has ever happened to me and now I wish it would. My life just goes on, one day after the other, and nothing happens. You have a 'north star,' if you know what I mean, a direction to go in. I was only wondering . . ."

Her voice trailed off and she couldn't hold onto the

thought. Maybe it was late and she was exhausted. Before she fell into the final shutoff of sleep though, she had a glimpse of the answer. Knowing that the *satori* or enlightenment was there, something she had only vaguely suspected before, could be the first step. This gave her a moment's turning of hope, and then sleep misted it out.

Elizabeth had no idea how long she had been sleeping when Maija shook her carefully and whispered in her ear. "Quiet, Liz, wake up but don't move. Lift your head very slowly. That's it, just like that."

Panic churned her vitals. Half-asleep, she envisioned a state trooper standing there, legs apart, in full uniform, pointing a gun at her. She looked up slowly and gasped in surprise. A herd of horses stood motionless in the moonlight behind the fence, twenty or thirty of them, perhaps more. Not a single sound or movement disturbed the quiet as they looked at Maija and her.

A chill passed through her, not of cold nor fear, but in answer to the incredible beauty of the waiting horses. For five, perhaps ten minutes or more, the horses stared at them, and the girls watched the moonlight shimmer along their flanks and long flowing manes. A long silence. Then the horse who must have been the leader tossed his head, turned, and galloped away. The other horses followed across the flat pasture land. Their hoofbeats, thunderous at first, grew fainter and fainter as the herd disappeared in the distance.

Once Elizabeth had seen an ancient Chinese screen in which a herd of horses stood in the moonlight. The horses on that screen and these were the same. Time had lost its meaning.

She turned to Maija and saw that her eyes were

shining too. The girls lay silently, completely awake. In an odd way, Elizabeth felt as though she had just been born. The next moment she fell into a dreamless sleep.

# 16

"It can't be this freezing!" Elizabeth said when she woke up the next morning and saw her breath. Shivering, she burrowed deeper into the sleeping bag while Maija jumped up and down to keep warm, mumbling something in a language Elizabeth didn't understand.

"There's even ice on top of the fence," Maija said. "We'd better get up and move before we become frozen statues."

"As if you weren't already up! Ugh, this is not easy," Elizabeth said, gritting her teeth and getting out of the sleeping bag. She hoped that this morning Maija would forego her early weaving stint, and fortunately, Maija did just that, buckling up the sleeping bag in record time so that they could get started. But, as Elizabeth knew, Maija began every day with weaving of one sort or another — "it's my way of becoming alive!" — and even now Maija picked up a flat stone from the road and stopped a moment to pull a ball of orange yarn from her pack. She put it in her pocket and then, scarcely losing a step, she walked on as swiftly as before while her fingers knotted, crocheted, worked and worried the wool around the stone. Elizabeth, blowing smoke rings in the cold air, watched the stone getting covered, no longer surprised at anything Maija would do.

Ravenously hungry, Maija let Elizabeth talk her into having pancakes and syrup at the next restaurant.

"The first thing I'm going to do when I get home, Maija, is take a long steaming hot bath and stay in it for an hour. I love baths, and bath oils, and bubble baths and hot steaming water. And then . . ."

A natural reticence gave way and Elizabeth began to talk about home. Even after they finished breakfast and went to the highway, she found herself talking about Sacramento. Surprisingly, Rick, Ken and Linda hardly came into the conversation; instead she spoke about her mother and her little sister, and she wondered if they still had Chess, the striped cat who would be fourteen years old now. She described the long grassy backyard of their house and the big basket-chair swing that hung from the tree there, and how she used to curl up and sit alone swinging and dreaming for hours. Mostly she talked about her mother, how dear and how unlike anyone else she was, and how exciting it always was when everyone in the family dressed up to go see Mother in the opening night of a new play.

Maija was fascinated. "I can hardly imagine anyone having a childhood like that. Storybook stuff. My own . . ." she sighed and smiled, "was a little different. Believe me."

Rides had thinned, and it was still cold. The girls jumped up and down, Maija crocheting around the stone the whole time. They could run in place, Maija suggested, but Elizabeth said she'd feel such a fool doing that if a car should come by. Finally a car stopped for them, a long luxurious Lincoln with two attractive men in the front seat. It even backed up so that they wouldn't have to run to it. The young men seemed gracious enough and Elizabeth was feeling ripples of excitement when Maija, just about to get in, stopped short and then stepped back.

"Thanks very much, but I don't think we'll leave until later," she said sweetly, offering no explanation for her sudden change of mind. Taking Elizabeth's hand she began to walk toward town. The men suddenly changed. They shouted obscenities at the girls, and the car sped away with a nasty spray of exhaust.

"Well, I like that! What's the big idea?" Elizabeth asked. "I thought they were nice. And I'm freezing, waiting here."

"You heard what they called us when they left. You call that *nice*?" Maija said. "Don't worry, there's always another ride. Always."

"But why did you pass them up? I don't understand you, Maija."

"Try to understand this. Just as I was about to get in, I felt a kind of chill going all the way down my spine, like that, one wave, and that one wave said *Don't Do It*. Just like that. So I didn't."

"You mean you have a little voice that tells you what to do and what not to do," Elizabeth said with a faint touch of scorn. She was freezing and Maija had just turned down a ride for apparently no reason at all.

"That's it exactly," Maija said, disregarding Elizabeth's lack of belief. Sometimes Maija sounded like a teacher, and in spite of herself, Elizabeth listened respectfully, like a disciple to a guru. "You have a knife in your boot, Liz. I know some karate and self-defense. But the best weapon of all is awareness, knowing what the other fellow is going to do. We're all born with it, like a sixth sense, but it gets educated out of us fast with too many 'should's' and 'shouldn'ts.' So we have to learn it all over again."

"But how did you know those men were dangerous? Did you see a gun or anything?"

"No. It looked fine. I suppose I could be wrong. But I felt prickles at the back of my neck, like the way a dog's hair stands up on end when he's scared. And when this happens, I trust it."

"How do you get this sixth sense, or whatever it is?"

Maija undid a row of knots on the stone and began to make them again, thinking all the while. Finally she spoke. "What a question! Sixth sense is only part of a big enormous awareness you get when you're in touch with your center. Centered. You need to find that very stillness deep within you, like the part in the very center of the wheel that doesn't move. Then everything will begin to fall in place. You'll begin to understand patterns in your life that you can't see literally but which are there.

"Liz, you don't believe a word I'm saying, do you? It's all right. Don't frown so. Someday you'll know what it's about. Anyway, it *was* only a ride, you know."

And as she spoke, another car, not as grand as the Lincoln, pulled up. This time Maija jumped in without hesitation, and Elizabeth followed quickly.

# 17

No sooner had the car taken off than Maija pulled out her stone and returned to her weaving; Elizabeth watched. The driver, a businessman Elizabeth would have guessed, was pleasant enough but hardly talkative, and after an easy exchange of words with Maija, was content to drive silently.

Maija's fingers knotted the yarn deftly, sometimes pulling it apart into fine strands so that a network of slender lines combined with thicker areas. In some places she wound the yarn around itself to make a strong cable. When she did not like a certain area, she pulled it out without hesitation and began that part over again. Working without stopping, she sometimes looked up to wink or smile at Elizabeth, amused at the way she waited for each new development. When the driver let them off, Maija concentrated on finishing the intricate covering while Elizabeth thumbed for rides.

"All the work you do is so beautiful! But I don't understand; why waste it on a plain brown stone?"

"I don't think it's wasted. I'm celebrating the stone. Just think, this stone was probably here before we were born and it will probably be here after we die. Think about that!"

"I'm afraid I just don't see it. What is there to celebrate?"

"That's your guess as well as mine. It's not all that important. This is a kind of mirror; that is, you think about it and it becomes what you think it is. Some Africans, for example, think there is a spirit in everything, even a stone like this, so they'd understand. Maybe I'm making an amulet out of it, something to ward off the evil eye. Maybe it's the joy of the work that makes it all worthwhile, and the stone is the heavy, somber thing that sets it off. Maybe the whole thing is simply absurd, going to all this trouble to dress up a stone. It's all how you look at it."

"I don't know what to think, Maija. I've never met anyone like you."

A car stopped for them and for the next half-hour Elizabeth sat in complete silence, musing. When they got out, she said, "Now I know what it makes me think of. You won't get mad if I tell you?"

"Do you think I would get angry when you're honest?"

"No, not really. You are the most gentle person ever, Maija. My theory . . . please don't laugh . . . is what I call the Ugly Baby Theory. Once I saw a very homely baby in front of a supermarket. I'd never seen such a homely baby in my life, and I wondered how the mother must have felt having to bring it up. But when she picked it up out of the carriage, it was dressed in a long dress with lace and bows, a hand-crocheted sweater and a charming, sort of silly but pretty bonnet, just as though it were the most beautiful baby in the world. In a way it was pathetic because the baby was still awfully homely, but all the beautiful clothes with the tucks and embroidery and lace made it important. Or maybe the mother cared so much for the baby that it showed through. Anyway, I guess I was impressed, because this happened well over a year ago, and I still remember it clearly. So your stone is like that, important and lovable because you've put this handsome garment around it. That's it. You don't think that's a dumb thing to say?"

Maija kissed her on both cheeks. "It's a beautful thing to say. Just beautiful. And so, for that you can have it, and we'll call it Ugly Baby."

Elizabeth held it in her hand, and then slipped it in her pocket so that now and then she could touch Ugly

Baby that wasn't really ugly, but blessed because Maija had made it so.

# 18

When rides were slow, they walked. All the hurry about getting to Sacramento dissolved in the clear fresh air and the ease of being with Maija. Time itself had changed, had grown less tense. Now there was more than enough.

"You don't mind if I ask you personal questions, do you, Maija? I mean, you could ask me anything at all and I wouldn't mind. Like, were you ever married? Are you married now? Would you like to be?"

"It's okay to ask. I was married once, when I was sixteen. It lasted for all of three weeks." Maija chuckled. "Sixteen. You're sixteen. Do you think it's a crazy age? No? Well, it seemed a good thing at the time. Randy was a toolmaker and made good money. It meant I could leave home; one less for Mom to feed and more room for the rest of the kids. I was already going to college even while I was in high school. Only, Randy had different ideas, such as going out and drinking beer every night. And sex, all that sex. And if I said, 'Hey, Randy, I have to study; I've got a midterm,' he would answer that we were married and what the hell did I need to go to school for. Etcetera. So one night I picked up my books to go to the library and bam, down the stairs came my other books, my clothes, my underwear, even my pots and pans. So I went home. End of marriage. Poor Randy never did figure it out."

"Would you want to get married again?"

"Someday. But it has to be the right man; I guess that's a silly expression. Someone I get along with, that's better. Anyway, I'm not in a hurry because what's in my mind is much more exciting than marriage."

She had to stop explaining because a car stopped for them. It took them forty miles closer to home, and when they got out the afternoon was so buttercup pleasant with the sky full of puffy clouds and the sun shining, that they walked across a field and lay down in the new spring pasture. It tickled, and Maija pulled out a long stalk and sucked on it. In the distance a herd of sheep moved slowly as they grazed.

Maija looked up at the skies and mused so long that Elizabeth thought she had changed her mind about telling her the exciting thing that was more important than marriage. Elizabeth had to wait; it *was* a little like being with a teacher.

"You know about weaving, Liz? It was one of the first marks of civilization when man could put fibers together to make a piece of cloth. In time they made symbols and pictures out of it, tapestries. You've seen them in museums, haven't you, big wide pictures? We haven't been making them like that for a long time, because the machine took over; and besides people could paint if they wanted a picture. But weaving still has a magic. Our fingers seem to need it and now weaving is coming back because people have a *need* to do it. It's like people needing to have gardens even though they can buy all the vegetables and fruit they want at the supermarket.

"So there's been a whole new interest in tapestry. Naturally, the designs used on the flat wall tapestries are very different from those done in the past, and they should be, because life is different. Also, people are finding new ways of using yarns and fibers, making it like sculpture. It's very exciting.

"So now we come to what I'm thinking. Imagine this, Liz. A place in the woods or on top of a hill, maybe not too far from the ocean. A workshop for anywhere from six to twelve people, where they can make enormous tapestries for important buildings, because the kind of architecture we have now needs large warm designs to cover the cold cement walls. Anyway, there's a need for big tapestry. And of course we'll have separate buildings too, perhaps small houses in the woods where artists can work by themselves on their own personal projects. We'll call it The Studio.

"Where will you find the artists to work with you? Are there enough?"

"I think so. So many people are getting into weaving. But we'll have to find artists who can get along with each other; working on large tapestries will take lots of cooperation. Everyone would be responsible for a certain amount of upkeep, too, like working in the garden or making the meals. I suppose once a year we could take on students for a few months to make money and also train future workers for ourselves."

"But Maija, it would be so expensive to find a place, and get the land and the looms and all the wool. What are you going to do about that?" No sooner had she said it, than she felt like biting her tongue. She was being practical, just like her father, and here was Maija dreaming of her utopia.

92

"Money will come of its own accord. We'll need a grant to get us started; and then there'll be commissions from banks, factories, large companies. We'll have to convince a few people that cold concrete walls need warm coverings, not because they're physically cold, but because they give a cold appearance. I already know one influential man who will help us out and he'll find others."

Clouds passed by. A single bird rose in the air and sang a song, then disappeared.

"It's more than a matter of just putting out work. It will be a way of living, by ourselves, in ourselves and with each other. The work itself is a way of living and that's why I don't worry about the money. If the people are right, if the work is right, money will take care of itself."

Elizabeth looked at her earnestly now. "I wish I could be part of it. It sounds like such a wonderful way to live."

"Well, why shouldn't you be part of it?"

"I don't know. I can't do anything to begin with. And there are other things." She mustn't forget, she reminded herself, that she was going back to Sacramento, to Rick, to her mother, to another kind of life entirely. Besides, she didn't know the first thing about weaving. She had made a potholder once, and that was the extent of her experience.

The afternoon grew warm, and when Elizabeth closed her eyes for a minute, she fell asleep. When she woke ten minutes later, she found that Maija had been sketching pictures of her in a pocket notebook. When Elizabeth asked to see them, she was allowed one quick glimpse, and then Maija closed the book.

# 19

They were getting closer to home. Utah. Nevada. At Winnemucca they were picked up by a wig salesman, full of jokes and stories. The girls laughed politely at his jokes, and Maija acted straight man for his comedy routine. He insisted on taking them to lunch. Afterwards, when the girls climbed back in the car, he asked, "Do you girls want to have some fun?"

"So this is it," Elizabeth thought. What had gone wrong with Maija's little voice that told her what to do? Silence.

"What's the matter? Awwww, you girls have it all wrong. You think I'm fresh? No, listen, I've got a lot of sample wigs in back there on the seat, can't use 'em anymore. I thought you'd have fun trying them on."

"That would be marvelous," Elizabeth said.

As they passed through the arid landscape, Maija laughed at herself in a wig of blonde curls and Elizabeth found a dense black wig with bangs.

"Wait a minute. That's incredible, Liz. It changes you so much; I wouldn't recognize you in it." Their laughter stopped as they looked thoughtfully at each other. Elizabeth recovered first, laughing again.

"Well, you're incredible in that. I mean, I just can't see you as a floozy, and there you are!"

"That's just what wigs are for. A change!" the salesman said.

They tried themselves as redheads, sleek strawberry blondes, platinum sirens, and finally, to Maija's incredible delight, she donned a harsh fall of auburn curls, the rattiest most ridiculous hairpiece she had ever seen.

"I could use this in a tapestry. Oh, I have just the place for it!"

"Take it, dear, take it! And you take one too, Elizabeth. A souvenir of our ride together. You're nice girls. I don't ask personal questions. But I can see, you are good girls. Intelligent."

They thanked him profusely, and after trying on all the wigs, Elizabeth settled on the straight black-haired one she had tried on first. Maija took the wild auburn curls. In almost no time at all they arrived in Reno. The salesman said he'd love to take them out for drinks, but he had "a certain little person waiting for him." They thanked him and he wished them good luck.

"You know, Maija, if I look so different in the wig, perhaps I ought to wear it. Someone might be looking for me in California."

"You're almost home now. But some other time you might really want it; it's a perfect disguise. We ought to think up a new name for you too."

They walked through the streets of Reno and after a glass of root beer at the A & W, Maija came up with the name.

Wanda Byrd. A wandering bird. Elizabeth laughed, passed by a mirror and touched her hand to her new black hair. It was a nervous laugh, for it was not just her name that was changing. In some deep and subtle way, she felt herself no longer the same.

# 20

The next ride was slightly out of the way, but it took them over Mount Rose, and when they looked below and saw Lake Tahoe sparkling like a long aquamarine jewel, Elizabeth begged Maija to stop and spend the night there. It was a long time since she'd been at Lake Tahoe and she wanted to love it all over again.

They slept under tall pines that stretched to the skies, and the next morning they sat by the lake while Maija finished the belt she had begun working on the night before.

"Let's stay another night! I love this place so much," Elizabeth begged.

"I thought you couldn't wait to get back," Maija said. "I'm tempted, too, but if that job is open, I'd better get to the city quick. Sorry."

After lunch a small and extremely pleasant lady, a professor's wife who was an ecologist, gave them a ride in a minibus. As she discussed the trees and lakes with Maija, Elizabeth found herself spellbound by the old familiar journey from the top of the Sierras down through the mountains and hills and foothills into the Great Central Valley. She had made this trip so many times she thought she knew every turn of the road and every blue-green vista, yet it was all new again after a long absence. Tears moistened her eyes; the exile returning home. She was satisfied that her dreams in

Lincoln had not been falsely sentimental. She truly loved her home, and this wide curving road was part of it.

They arrived in Sacramento a little after four that afternoon, and the kind lady let them off at the L Street parking lot. After the chill of Wyoming and the night mountain air, the valley heat was overpowering, even though Elizabeth knew this weather was mild compared to the sauna heat that would be coming in June.

"The least I can do is get rid of this silly wig," Elizabeth said as she unpinned it. For a second she was tempted to throw it away, but on second thought put it in her pack.

Her excitement at being home began to mount. She had accomplished the wild impossible feat! And Sacramento looked so good!

"Even L Street looks good to me. I'm so glad to be home! Want to see the State Capitol? It's only a few blocks away."

"Sure. I won't be satisfied until I've seen it," Maija said, amused at Elizabeth's excitement. Now it was her turn to follow Elizabeth.

They strolled up the street, basking in its warmth. Elizabeth was surprised all over again to find that she was glad to see the State Capitol, which before had always looked to her like something flat, cut out of cardboard and propped up, like a drawing exercise. The park around the Capitol with its tall rows of palms, the evergreens and delicate pepper trees, filled her with joy.

"When I was a little girl, I used to think this was so grand. Then I thought it was kind of corny. But now, it's all grand again, only in a different way. Or maybe I like it because it's always been there."

Maija listened while Elizabeth said she simply must see a certain magnificent redwood tree on the grounds, and then she remembered the French ice cream shop where her mother used to take her. She would take Maija there and treat her to a Café Liegeois: she would love it! But when they got there, the building had been torn down and a new one was going up.

"Oh no! I wonder how much else this place has changed," Elizabeth said, disappointed. "But I know another place not too far away. Want to go there?"

As they sipped their sodas, a new awkwardness loomed for Elizabeth. Shouldn't she offer to take Maija home with her? Had her own father been there, she would have been proud to show off Maija, but she didn't know her new stepfather any too well. Her mother, who, she must remember, was now Mrs. Don Powell, might have a problem accepting her own daughter under the circumstances, and Maija's presence couldn't possibly help ease the situation.

Elizabeth, seeing Maija's reflection in the mirror over the ice cream bar, looked at her as though she had never seen her before. In the few days they had been together, Maija had taken on a "Maija-look" that to Elizabeth was beautiful. But Maija was not attractive in the usual magazine advertisement sense of the word. Of course, once she began to talk, none of that mattered. But Don Powell would never understand a free soul like Maija, and her mother would say, "Why doesn't she fix herself up a little?" The suggestion of a New Jersey accent, if that's what it was she had, and that unconventional cap of hers weren't going to impress anyone at home favorably. She would ask her some other time, after she'd been home a while.

They wandered back to the park, and Maija rummaged through her backpack. Finally, she pulled out the belt that was a "whatever" and gave it to Elizabeth.

"Perhaps you'll want to use it sometime."

"I can't take this, Maija. It's your *living*. Anyway, Maija, I have the Ugly Baby and I love it, and . . . I'd never forget this wonderful trip anyway."

"Please take it if you want it. For your velvet dress or your jeans. Whatever."

"But you were going to sell all your things. You'll need to pay rent and things like that."

Maija held up her hand. "I told you, money takes care of itself. And also, Liz, I want to give you my address. You might want to look me up sometime when you come to the city."

She wrote it on a page torn from a sketchbook; on the back was a curving abstract pencil sketch. Elizabeth thanked her and promised to come see her sometime.

"If you do a tapestry, I hope you'll let me see it. I really am curious about it now. I know you're going to be very famous, Maija. And you were so good to me, and for me. I don't know what I would have done without you."

With that, they reached a point of silence. Elizabeth, radiant at being home once more, felt a rush of guilt knowing that Maija would go on alone and that she had not once mentioned friends who would welcome her in San Francisco. She had once said that she would have to find a place to live, and now Elizabeth thought it must be dismal to have to go to the city without anyone to greet her. As the time of separating approached, Maija truly seemed less anxious to get to San Francisco.

"I hope it turns out the way you want it, Liz. Rick

and the red Porsche and the white bikinis and the blue swimming pools. And your mother will be overjoyed to see you, don't worry about that."

"And I hope everything works out for you too, the job and new friends and all that. San Francisco is such a great place to live," Elizabeth said.

It was awkward now, using words when there was nothing left to say. Elizabeth saw a bus go by and picked up her backpack. "If they haven't changed the schedule, my bus comes in less than five minutes, and if I miss it, I have to wait an hour and a half."

With that, the girls gathered their gear and walked over to the bus stop.

Maija tried to smile. Elizabeth tried to hide her joy. Even the smelly old bus she had always hated looked precious as it hissed to a stop in front of them. The girls hugged each other tightly, as though they didn't want to part. Maija, more controlled, broke away first, telling Elizabeth she mustn't miss the bus and Elizabeth scrambled on just in time. As the bus pulled away, their glance held and it seemed to Elizabeth that Maija looked very, very alone.

# III
# Sacramento

# 21

As the bus rumbled on through the old familiar streets, the last eight days faded away like a dream. In time, Elizabeth thought, she might wonder if they had ever happened at all, so out of context were they with the rest of her life. Every block yielded memories. Fine old homes had been turned into offices and apartment buildings. Farther out of town she found the same golden harp in the window that she had always looked for when she was a child going past on the bus, and in the next block the dovecote was still there, and farther on the same grove of high bamboo was intact. As simply as that, Elizabeth Wanda Byrd returned to being Elizabeth van Vliet. Her childhood rose within her. She was home once more.

She jumped off the bus at the familiar bus stop and walked down the street where she had always lived, even cutting across the curve in the road in the same old way. It wasn't until she found an unfamiliar young woman in yellow shorts fussing around a petunia bed in front of the old white brick house that she remembered it wasn't her home anymore. This low gracious house with the towering oaks taller than ever, so dignified after Lorene's plastic-rose cottage, this house, where she had lived since she was a baby, was no longer hers or her mother's or her father's. Her parents had sold it when her mother married Don Powell.

Elizabeth had learned of the sale in one of her mother's letters, and had found it difficult to believe. Now she saw with her own eyes that it really did belong to someone else, a stranger, the woman in the yellow shorts. The place looked altered in some way. Elizabeth soon realized what it was: her father's camellia trees, of which he had been so proud, had been replaced with common evergreens. Poor Dad! She would never tell him.

She lingered by the oleander bushes that bordered the yard, breathing in their sweet fragrance. Once she had taken them for granted; now the full bushes with their dark green leaves and generous white blossoms seemed like miracles. Two small girls, hair light as milkweed silk, pulled a wagon onto the front lawn while a small poodle frisked and yipped around them. Lawn, children, trees, flowers, the dog, even the lady fussing with her petunias . . . all were bathed in the streaming late afternoon sunlight. She was a visitor in a museum looking at a picture in a frame.

"It might have been Mark and me playing there, just like that, not so very long ago," she thought. She could almost see her mother in a long, shimmery, blue-green silk dress coming to the front door and calling that it was time for dinner in that fake Irish accent she liked to use. Her mother with the thick waves of black hair, always possessing a touch of wildness, never perfect, the intense Irish blue eyes and the white skin. A beautiful woman, a little too full perhaps, a little sloppy, but smelling of subtle perfumes. Before dinner they would linger on the brick patio in the back of the house, martinis for the parents and ginger ale in wine glasses for the children. Her father, all quietness and reserve, would sit back in his chair and smile at his wife who was always moving and talking and gesturing, an actress without cessation. When she was in a play, she became that character, and when she wasn't given a part, she made up her own for her audience at home. She could be Lady Whatsis, Mrs. Pee-tee-aye, Starlet Scarlet or Mucky Maude, sending her audience into hysterics. Her father would smile and shake his head, wondering, as he often said, where such a woman came from.

The sweetness of those days came flooding back. The first anger and shock at the divorce announcement had long ago given way to an unanswerable why and then to a final acceptance. Now her acceptance was ripped open, and Elizabeth could only ask why once again. Why had her mother been so foolish; how could her father have been so self-righteous and stubborn? Couldn't they guess whàt they were going to lose?

"Are you looking for someone? Can I help you?"

The young mother had come over to Elizabeth, trowel in hand. She smiled civilly enough but her suspicion was unmistakable. It wasn't until Elizabeth saw herself in the mirror later on that she realized how strange she must have looked in that neighborhood.

"I'm afraid I have the wrong street," she mumbled. "Sorry."

And with that she walked away, heading for the new section, where her mother and Don Powell had bought a house.

# 22

In contrast to the old house, the new one showed itself pathetically — still raw, in the company of other new houses on a recently opened street. Some new houses promise a quality of mellowness to come with time, but this one suggested a look of sterility that would only intensify with age. Newly planted grass came up sparsely — had a first crop failed? — and the trees, thin sticks with the nursery labels still on, would be no match for the merciless valley sun.

"Poor Mother. She loved the other house so much. How can she stand this?" Elizabeth said to herself. And again she wondered how adults could rip up their lives so tragically.

She rang the bell at the front door and waited. Don Powell, older and puffier than Elizabeth remembered him, came to the door in shirt-sleeves, a newspaper dangling from one hand. Apparently she too looked different, for he did not recognize her.

"Yes?"

"Hello, Donald! Don't you recognize me? I'm Elizabeth."

"Well, I'll be —! My God, here she is. Hey, Mollie, she's here!"

Her mother, tears flying from her eyes and laughing with a relief near hysteria, came rushing down the stairs uttering incoherent cries. At the sight of her, emotions welled up in Elizabeth. She so loved her mother, yes, she did. Yet she noticed that her mother was dressed in a long emerald cocktail dress. So early?

Mollie's impulse to embrace her daughter was checked for the briefest moment. "I must look awful," Elizabeth thought. But it was only a moment, and then they were locked in each other's arms. The heady Lanvin scent of her mother's perfume, mixed with a certain personal fragrance arising from Mollie herself, was familiar and dear all over again.

"I really love her. I do, I do. I really love my mother!" the words sang.

"What a relief to see you! Are you all right? We'll have to call your father right away; he's been so worried. Where were you anyway? How did you get here? The police were looking out for you. Oh Liz, you're so *thin!* Too thin. Look at her, Don. She's so beautiful, isn't she? But thin. Are you hungry?"

"Just filthy, Mother. Really filthy. Starving too. A little. Otherwise fine. Oh Mom, I'm so glad to see you again."

She threw her arms around her mother again. Once more she loved the details that gave Mollie her unique appearance, the well-shaped hands that carried too many rings whether it was the fashion or not, the dress split up the sides in a fashion too daring and theatrical. Yet she carried it off. She had grown somewhat stouter and her hair had not lasted out its last dyeing job. All these things suddenly brought a touch of pity along with admiration. "I must love her and I will, I will," Elizabeth promised as she kissed her again.

"I'm sorry for the way I look, Mother, coming into your nice new house like this. I'd love a bath . . ."

"Well, of course! My lady of the bath! Remember you used to soak for hours! Oh Liz, I could look at you all night long. Look, Don, isn't she wonderful? Isn't it great to have her with us?"

"I'm looking at her all right," he said, and Elizabeth realized he had been doing just that, taking her in from head to dust-capped toe. "But look, Mollie dear, we ought to be on our way to the Randalls' right now . . ."

"Of course, darling. Wait, I have to fix my face. Be right down," she called, dashing up the stairs.

It was then that Elizabeth noticed the little girl in the shorts and soft yellow jersey, who had been standing by and watching.

"Penny! It's not you! You're so grown-up!"

She knelt and hugged her sister warmly. The narrow face with the wide gray eyes and high forehead, the long pale hair and slender legs were familiar, "like meeting myself as a child once more" she thought.

"Do you remember me, Penny?"

"Sure, Liz. Are you going to stay with us now?"

"I don't know yet. But I'll be here for a little while anyway. It's so good to see you!"

"Mollie, get a move on!" Don roared up the stairs.

Elizabeth, supposing she should say something to him after bursting in and paying no attention to him at all, held out her hand and smiled. He pointed to his cheek and she pecked it dutifully. In turn he kissed her — too warmly, Elizabeth felt — but she was able to break away when she saw her mother coming down the stairs.

"Honey, let's call your father and let him know you've come. Poor man, he's so worried. And I want to show you your room. I wish I could stay home . . ."

"Not tonight, Mollie. Liz can call her father herself,

you don't have to do it, and Penny will show her where to sleep. There's steak in the freezer, Liz, so help yourself to that. Mollie, for heaven's sake . . ."

"It's all right, Mom. I can take care of myself. Don's in a hurry," Elizabeth said, and then she noticed that her mother's dress wasn't completely hemmed.

"Oh Mother, you're just the same. Your hem is coming down. I'd better fix it. I can do it in a minute."

"Oh dear, what would I do without you? I forgot. It came down the last time I wore it and I had to use Scotch Tape on it. Donnie, love, it won't take a minute. Penny, angel, will you bring the sewing box?"

It was old times all over again. Elizabeth sat on the floor and concentrated on making the tiny, even stitches such a dress deserved while her mother turned slowly.

"You know, Liz, you gave us such a scare. We worried that you were hitch-hiking. Naughty girl! You could have been murdered or raped. Look, I'm just going to call your father."

She reached for the phone which had a long extension wire and dialed the number, which, Elizabeth noticed, she knew by heart. In the meanwhile Don, who had started for the car, yelled at them to hurry. Elizabeth heard the phone ring eight times before her mother sighed and hung up.

"No one home. Liz, dear, will you call him yourself later tonight, then?" her mother asked. Don was now blowing the horn impatiently, so Mollie blew kisses to both the girls and rushed out.

"Well, Penny, that leaves you and me. And I've got to have a bath right away."

"Can I watch?"

108

"Sometime we'll take a bath together. But right now I'm too dirty from the long trip. Let's have dinner together afterward. How's that?"

"I've had mine. But I'll have more dessert."

"We'll have a wonderful time. And you can tell me all about school and your new friends."

Elizabeth dawdled in a steaming bath, luxuriating in her mother's bath oils. Clouds of the bubble bath which Penny had insisted on giving her obscured the new lean hardness of her body. Bit by bit she relaxed and her eyes closed. Too many conflicting emotions drove out all the daydreams she had had about her homecoming for almost a year.

She would have to call Rick, but maybe tomorrow was soon enough. First she would have to call her father, and that would hardly be easy. She lay back in the tub; "Where was Maija now?" she wondered. Already the long trip was slipping into the past.

A timid knock on the door, the door slowly opened, and Penny's golden head poked in. "Want me to dry you?"

"Sure, honey, if you like."

And so the evening went by, not in the least as it was planned, but somehow satisfying. After dinner, Elizabeth followed Penny to her room.

"Let's play."

Two shelves full of dolls sat new and unplayed with, but Penny had found an old erector set Mark had left behind.

"See, I've made a tower and a truck, but this darn bridge won't work!" she complained, frustrated.

"Let's see if I can figure it out," Elizabeth said, studying the diagram. "There must be a way. Don't worry, Penny, we'll get it."

"Good heavens, what am I doing," she asked herself, never once having been tempted to play with a mechanical set. What audacity to think she could do it! Penny sat with large gray eyes fixed on her, seeming relieved and confident that her big sister would know what to do.

"All right. First we take this apart and see just how many pieces we have," Elizabeth said, trying to sound as though she knew all about it. She worked deliberately, concentrating hard, and was grateful to Penny for whatever discoveries she was making in the process. In a little over two hours, the bridge stood complete.

"Look! Hooray for us!" she cried, hugging Penny.

"We did it! We did it! Let's do another one now, huh, Liz?"

"Now? Ten-thirty? Hmm, not tonight. Some other time."

"Promise?"

"Promise."

When at last Penny was in bed, tucked under a thin yellow blanket, she threw her arms around Elizabeth and said, "Don't ever go away again, will you? I like it when you're home. Please Liz. Stay here."

A flash of poor homely Patty alone in the dull bedroom Elizabeth had left behind rose to contrast with Penny's silken hair spreading over the pillow. Penny and everything around her spoke of luxury, especially the bouquet of yellow roses, undoubtedly her mother's doing, in a small silver pitcher, and the antique doll on the ivory-painted bedside table. Yet maybe her sister needed her too, she thought. More than Patty?

"I'll stay if I can, Penny. We have to see how things

110

work out. If it's possible, I'll do it. And now, pleasant dreams. Goodnight, little darling."

# 23

The valley sun slanted through the louvres in brilliant stripes and woke Elizabeth, who lay in bed, lazy and yawning. Satisfied to sleep between clean sheets, to wake to the sun, take a morning bath, and then go downstairs to sit with Mother for almost two hours while they talked over coffee and rolls . . . it was heaven.

"I ought to call Rick," she said, wondering why she wasn't in more of a hurry.

"Good lord, did you call your father last night? What did he say, Liz?"

"He still wasn't home. Let's call him now."

Elizabeth was touched by her mother's eagerness to speak with her father again, and she stood by while her mother dialed the number. Mollie, bubbling as she spoke, seemed much like the old Mollie, as she explained joyfully that Elizabeth was found and, when he became angry about her hitch-hiking, soothed him with a philosophic, "All's well that ends well, dearie." Finally with some reluctance, she gave the telephone to Elizabeth.

"Are you all right Elizabeth? You have taken ten years off my life."

"I'm sorry, Dad. Yes, I'm fine. And how are you?"

She felt all his suffering traveling over the wires, the worry, the tension, the hurt, the anger and the relief because she was all right. "Please don't worry. I didn't mean to upset you." How she wanted to comfort him, but Lorene's children were being noisy in the background and she guessed he wasn't free to talk as he would have liked.

"If I write to you, Dad, will you answer? I'd like to explain a little."

"Please do. Liz, send the letters to my office and try to keep your head on your shoulders. No more hitchhiking. You understand?"

"I promise, Dad. And, give my love to Mark. And Patty. I love you too."

"All right, Elizabeth. Goodbye now. Remember to write."

She could have wept at the restraint in his voice. She could feel his mouth held in a tense line and knew he would probably go out in his car after hanging up because he would want to be alone for awhile.

They hung up. She turned to her mother, both of them relieved and a little sad. Then her mother brightened. "Let's go shopping and get you some clothes!"

Elizabeth's mother bought her a light casual coat, a bikini, a white piqué dress, and finally a pale shirt. Elizabeth noted that her mother stopped to look at the price tags first, something she had never done before, and she wondered if Don were strict with her about money.

Over lunch, while the marshmallow music of Muzak softened everything inside the restaurant and outside the hot sun screamed on the pavement, Elizabeth asked her mother about the theater, hoping she would find a rush of sparkle, enthusiasm or even gossip. But her mother smiled sadly.

"I haven't been doing too much. Times have changed, you know," she spoke like an actress reciting the lines of a play, but Elizabeth knew her better. It was genuine. "I've been past leading roles for a long time, but I've always done character parts, you know, and I do them well. It's not conceit; it's the truth. This year they gave me a little bone now and then, two or three lines, and that's it. Liz, it isn't fair. I've been acting all my life."

"And you're good too. There was always a kind of magic about you once you hit the stage."

"Do you really think so? Liz, you're such a comfort, you know. My life seems to have been chopped off . . . but I shouldn't talk about such things. Look, here are our salads. And you can have my mayonnaise," she said virtuously.

"Isn't this nice, Elizabeth, having lunch the way we used to? Oh, I do hope you'll stay with us. We'll go to the city, go and see some *good* theatre. And you can get back to your friends again . . ."

"But Mother, are you sure you have room at home? If I stay in Don's study, that will crowd him out."

"He won't mind. It was supposed to be a guest room anyway. And he thinks you're awfully cute, so there's no problem there. I don't know what it was like in Lincoln, but I know we want you here with us now."

Elizabeth tried not to notice that she was asking her to stay, much as Penny had begged last night. If her mother was becoming the child, was she, Elizabeth, willing to become *Mollie's* mother?

Mollie still seemed on the verge of pleading, though she tried to smile, and Elizabeth reached across the table and squeezed her hand. Comforting her, Elizabeth knew that she had in some way grown up.

# 24

Sunning brought on dreaming. Later that afternoon, Elizabeth lay on a towel in the backyard, letting the sun toast her to a golden brown. She dreamed of Maija and wished she were there, and yet she couldn't even imagine her in such a setting. The luxury of home was a comfort, but it wouldn't make up for everything.

"My mind isn't working right yet," she thought, getting up to go in the house. She wasn't ready for a large dose of the Valley sun yet.

On the way upstairs to shower and change, she heard a familiar voice on the TV, so she stopped to look.

"Come on down to Bargain Bob's and git yourself a bargain to-day!" Bargain Bob! She had, mercifully enough, forgotten him. Rick's father, dressed in a loud checkered shirt and straw hat and using a hackneyed imitation of a hillbilly or farmer, was still acting out commercials with two other car dealers. Their home-made dramatic efforts led them to imitate jockeys, football players or members of a band. Their soft paunches protruded through every disguise; their vaguely southern accents seemed invariably the same; and their little plays showed such poverty of imagination and so little human dignity that Elizabeth, who had always laughed at them before with everyone else, now found herself shuddering. Looking at Rick's father, she remembered clearly what Rick looked like, and now she knew what he would become.

"Well, you enjoying the California sun?"

Donald had come into the room and put his hand on her bare shoulder. Instinctively she moved back and held the towel up in front of her. He felt the rebuff.

"You surprised me!" she said, trying to laugh it off. "The sun is fine, but I guess I've had a little too much of it. I was on my way to take a bath."

She told herself he was only being courteous. After all, she was a guest in his house, but he picked up the newspaper as though her reaction were a matter of indifference.

"As you like," he said.

Later she called Rick. After all, she told herself, it wasn't fair to put him in his father's place. With luck he might turn out differently after all.

"Heeeeeeello!" She had almost forgotten his long drawn out way of answering the telephone. When she saw him again, everything would fall into place and be like it was before.

"Hello, Rick. How are you?"

"Who is this?" A slight impatience in his voice.

"You don't know, Rick?"

"Elizabeth?" Hesitation turned to excitement. "Liz, it isn't you?"

She laughed. "That's who."

"Where are you? You callin' from Lincoln?" He talked louder, which amused Elizabeth, as though she were actually back there.

"I'm here. Sacramento."

"Well, how about that!"

After a long conversation with awkward pauses, he invited her to a party that night.

"Thanks, but it's not your party and I wasn't invited."

"Cindy won't mind. This will be a big party and you can meet some new kids there. You'll like 'em. I'll stop by for you about nine. Okay?"

"You're sure it's all right?"

"I wouldn't ask you if it wasn't. Hey, where you living now?"

When she put down the receiver later, she hardly knew what to think. It was Rick, but it didn't seem like Rick. Was he different or was she? Linda and Ken had broken up. So much for reviving old times!

At nine she was waiting, dressed in a long blue dress with a halter top. She tried on Maija's belt but it was too elegant, so she put the intricate weaving away. Perhaps she would hang it on the wall in front of her so she could see it each morning when she woke up.

At nine-thirty she was still waiting and about to give up, when a horn blew and a minute later Rick was at the door. He kissed her, but it was a brotherly kiss. They were as awkward as if they hadn't met before.

It was a shock to see a small black sports car in front. "What happened to the Porsche?"

"Oh, that! It got totaled last January. Absolute wreck."

"Oh Rick, what a shame! I loved that car."

"Yeah, but life goes on just the same. Right, Liz?"

The second surprise was Cheryl, a cool, pretty girl with curly black hair sitting in the front seat. So that was it! Elizabeth had a terrible desire to laugh, and in fact she did giggle a little when Rick introduced the girls. Cheryl said hello distantly.

"Rick, I don't really want to crowd you two. I don't have to go."

"Yes you do, Liz." She wondered if he had already

116

been drinking. "You'll have a wonderful time and Cheryl and I like being crowded. Ha, ha!"

Elizabeth stepped into the car and found herself laughing. Rick acted as if he thought her drunk or more likely a little daft. He'd always told her that she was "different" anyway.

"Well, what's so funny?" Cheryl asked her, clearly disgusted.

Immediately Elizabeth stopped. To have dreamed of Rick all year and then to have discovered that she did not care if he had a Cheryl or a thousand new friends and that it would not matter to her if she never saw him again . . . well, why not laugh about it! Maija would understand that it was funny; Maija alone would understand.

"Now I know I'm home. This is really it," she said half an hour later as she floated in the pool. The Japanese lanterns strung above made moving puddles of light in the water, and far above the party, almost forgotten, the deep night sky stayed cool and still. Fire leaped from the barbecue pit. The yard was full of young people; the girls in long cotton dresses, flashes of light displaying the wild colors, and the young men, talking, singing, and sometimes bursting into loud fits of laughter. Now and then a combo played, raw music drowning out everything else. A noisy party is supposed to be a good party.

"Hey, Liz is home. Did you know that? She's in the pool."

"No kidding! I'm going to find her."

She had not thought of Allen once during the year, but he found her and they embraced. Other friends came, Toni, Erica and Gina. How good it was to see them! Maybe it was just as well the old quartet was over. Starting fresh was the best way after all.

"I'll race you three laps across the pool." A new young man she had never met before swam up to her with easy grace.

They didn't race but swam four laps together and afterward sat on the edge of the pool while he covered her with a terry robe. His name was Reggie and he was handsome, intelligent most likely, and admiration for her shone in his eyes.

"It's not a bad party," she remarked, wanting something to say and knowing better than to confess how wonderful it was. She had been starving for this all year, this California richness, the long pool and the garden that combined Japanese taste with California wealth. That the sparseness had cost thousands of dollars was inconsequential. She wanted only to enjoy it and to enjoy the people here.

"You know, California is really different. There isn't, there can't be, any other place like it. I had to come back," she told Reggie.

"But hitch-hiking, wow! You're really gutsy."

"Nothing to it. Pardon me. I'm getting cold. Think I'll get dressed."

"Liz, will you let me take you home later, when you're ready to leave?"

She laughed. "All right. That would be nice."

As she dried herself in the cedar dressing room, half-hidden under a Monterey pine, she thought, "It's going to work after all. And I won't have to ride home with Rick. I'm making new friends already!" When she came out, Reggie was waiting with a drink in his hand for her.

"No thanks. Not tonight."

"Oh come on. You know better than that."

The hostess saved her with a Coke, but there was scorn in the way she handed it to her. Everyone else was drinking. Elizabeth was not prepared for the elaborate bar, the number of girls laughing too shrilly and boys who had obviously helped themselves too generously. She wandered among the groups, and finally settled on the outside of one, but they were talking about classmates she didn't know. Reggie sneaked up behind her.

"A penny for your thoughts."

"They aren't worth it."

He gave her a pretzel and took a few himself; he led her through the garden walks.

"When I was little, I used to wish I were invisible so I could go to my mother's parties. Now I really do feel invisible," she said.

"You're not invisible to me, Liz. I've never been so overcome by such gorgeous visibility," he said. Party talk, pleasant but not to be taken seriously.

A burst of music from the combo blasted through the air, and Elizabeth moved away through the extensive grounds toward a rocky mound where water flowed, resembling a mountain stream. Contrived, yes, but so well-designed, it might have been transported from the Sierras. Then, in spite of the music still loud even there, retching sounds close by drew her attention. A boy was being sick over a shrub of apricot-colored azaleas. She turned to Reggie.

"I don't want to stay any longer. It's too early for you to take me home, so thanks anyway."

"Honey, you can't walk all that way. I promised I'd take you. If you don't wanna stay, then let's go."

"I don't want to spoil your good time. It's just that I've had it."

She said goodbye to her friends, thanked the hostess, waved to Rick, and was grateful to Reggie for taking her home in his yellow MG. She wasn't sure how she would have found the way, and because she needed new friends, it might be a good idea to begin with Reggie.

But he pretended to be lost, drove to a secluded bushy spot, parked the car, grabbed her and began to kiss her heavily, leaning against her.

"Please," she said pushing him away and thinking he had misunderstood her. "I really meant it about going home. I want to go straight home. "

"Liz, babe, it's early. You don' really wanna go home."

He grabbed her again. This time she became angry and stamped on his instep. He winced in pain, and she opened the door and began to run. He quickly followed her in his car.

"Liz, Elizabeth, come back. Please come back. I won't touch you, I promise."

She walked on, head high in the air.

"Come on, you like it. You know you like it. We can have lots of *fun* together. We're just right together. I'll take it easy with you."

She walked on silently and then panicked when he stepped on the gas and came so close to her that he almost ran her down. Then he turned around with a sickening scrape of tires and sped away.

She stopped to catch her breath and let her heart quiet down.

The walk home took her half an hour because she

wasn't sure where the new house was. It was just as well, since she needed time to think. On Monday, she decided, she would go to school, and this time she would make entirely new friends, bright ones, the ones who cared about what was happening in the world. Maybe somebody like Danny Wilson.

But her thoughts centered elsewhere. In the cool, dark quiet of the velvet night air, she saw the lone figure of Maija and found herself longing to see her.

# 25

It did not take quite two weeks to learn that Sacramento wasn't going to work out, but it took that long for Elizabeth to acknowledge it. Now where was she going to go? What was she going to do?

Though the party left a bitter taste, she had reasoned she would find other people at school, healthier, saner, and less decadent. She would join the groups and clubs she had so blithely ignored at Lincoln. But it was the end of the year and with vacation in sight, enthusiasm had waned. "Join us next fall," her new acquaintances urged.

Nor did things work out academically. "If only you had waited until June," the personnel administrator sighed. Her grades from Lincoln were excellent but incomplete, and her old courses did not correspond to those in the Sacramento school system.

"If I were you," the counselor said, "I'd go back to

Lincoln immediately and take the finals. Otherwise, you might lose a whole semester."

"I'll think about it," Elizabeth promised.

She planned to talk with her mother, heavy-hearted though she was about returning to Lincoln, but when she got home, her mother was fussing in the kitchen, getting dips and crackers ready and putting canapés together.

"Liz, I'm so glad you're here. Don invited some business associates over for cocktails. I could use some help, if you don't mind."

Her mother looked so unhappy that Elizabeth put her arm around her. Her mother who used to love any kind of party so much! Nothing was working anymore.

She dreaded the cocktail parties that Don seemed to like so well. This would be the third one since she'd been home, and the other two were miserable experiences. Don, wanting to show Elizabeth off, put his arm around her and introduced her as his daughter, while Mollie refilled the drinks and passed around the dips. Elizabeth smiled nervously and tried to break away, but Don held her firmly, and of course her mother saw it all.

Two mornings later, while her mother was upstairs on the extension phone, Don tiptoed up to Elizabeth and kissed her on the back of the neck while she was pouring orange juice for breakfast.

"Please, you mustn't do that," she whispered.

"Honey, we are related, you know. And I like having you around. Don't you want to be friends?"

He kissed her and she broke away. "What would my mother think if she saw you?"

"Well, what difference would it make?"

She picked up her books and ran off to school. That day she decided to swallow her pride and go back to Lincoln. All day long she found herself sighing heavily, and that night she cried herself to sleep. Going back wasn't the answer, not the answer she wanted.

# 26

Nevertheless, two days later it was all settled. She was going back. They had called her father, and he agreed it was the best thing to do. Don had taken everyone out to dinner the night before and presented Elizabeth with a check for the airfare, even though he let her know he took her departure as an insult. "What's a couple of grade points? So you graduate a semester later."

On the day she was to leave on an eleven-thirty plane, she sat with her mother at the breakfast table. They drank endless cups of coffee. He mother lit a cigarette, dabbed at her eyes with a sodden handkerchief, and tried to explain how much she loved Elizabeth.

"Mother," Elizabeth said, brimming over with distress. What had happened to her beautiful mother, the actress? "Mom, go see a psychologist or a therapist. Please. You'll feel so much better. And it's no disgrace."

Her mother lifted her head, still the actress. "I've been through rough waters before, and I've always come through. So don't worry, my dear. Don't worry about me. But I will be missing you, Liz. Sometimes I think women understand each other in a way that men never can."

"That could be true. I think so too," Elizabeth agreed, thinking of Maija.

Time had leaped ahead and Elizabeth got up with a cry. Time to go! She must get dressed and finish packing. The suitcase her mother had given her was filled with new and old clothes and although the backpack looked out of place over her new spring coat, she thought she'd need it anyway. Soon it all rested on the floor of the Mercury, and she sat beside her mother.

"We'll make it," Mollie cried, "so don't panic. I can really handle this car, especially if you don't mind speeding a little."

The car refused to start. Mollie tried it again, kicked it, pleaded with it, swore it was only flooded and then gave up. It was dead, stone dead.

"And the garage man will take hours to come," she moaned. "I know. It's happened before."

"I could take a taxi."

"Ha! They're slower than the mechanics," Mollie said.

They sat there so gloomily they hardly noticed the car backing out of the driveway across the street. Then Mollie came to life, jumping out of the car and waving, "Oh, Mrs. Trimble, Mrs. Trimble!"

She ran across the street, chatted with the lady in the car, and then ran back.

"What luck! It's Mrs. Trimble's day at the museum. She'll drop you off at the Senator Hotel and you can take the limousine to the airport!"

She helped put the luggage in Mrs. Trimble's car

while Elizabeth assured her she didn't have to go out to the airport with them. So they said goodbye, hurriedly, tearfully, intoning all the last-minute phrases of good luck, write, please write, let me know when you get there, and we'll be together soon again. Mollie waved sadly as Mrs. Trimble drove off.

Then Elizabeth was at the hotel waiting for the limousine. The more she waited the more she felt she shouldn't take the plane. It felt wrong. Maybe the plane was going to blow up and this was a forewarning. Maija had said more than once, a person must never do what feels wrong.

Was Lincoln the wrong place for her, an old snakeskin she had shed? Let it go, then. Sacramento was another skin she had shed, so she no longer fit there either. If only she didn't want her father and her mother so much; if only she didn't need them still; if only they didn't want her so much. And yet, neither her father nor mother wanted her enough to change their way of living so they could have her. Nobody wanted her very much, really.

Nobody? Nobody at all?

What about Maija? She remembered the last time she saw her, a small straight figure looking after her as the bus moved away. Well, she could at least go and see her. Maija had given her the address, so it meant she was expecting her sooner or later. This was sooner, but with Maija it would be all right. Nervously she looked through her wallet, hoping the address was still there; at last she found it, crushed to the bottom, but there. Elizabeth was unwrinkling it as the limousine pulled up to the hotel. She let it leave without her, as she hoisted the pack on her back and walked away.

Elizabeth stopped at a bank and cashed the check Donald had given her without too much difficulty. The money in her hand meant freedom. With her heart beating wildly, as if she were carrying out a criminal plan, she walked over to the Greyhound station a few blocks away and bought a one-way ticket to San Francisco.

"This has to be right," she convinced herself, "because I just couldn't go back to Nebraska. I couldn't."

As the bus pulled away, she thought of her poor father waiting for her in vain at the airport. She could see him phoning her mother to find out what had happened, her mother's chagrin, and Donald fuming with anger. Should she send a telegram to her father to let him know she was all right? Of course not. He'd have her picked up in no time. Someday she'd go back to him, but not yet, not quite yet. "If I am becoming hard," she thought, "too bad. That's the way it is. Tough. Sometimes it's only the hard who survive."

The sun-gold hills of the valley were changing to the cool blue of the coast as the bus neared San Francisco. How surprised Maija would be and how delighted! Of course she'd be delighted. Elizabeth imagined arriving to find her working in a studio. She would turn to see her, the dark eyes shining, then rush to greet her. A jubilation, like the singing of the Hallelujah Chorus.

Why, there was no question; this was where she belonged. Yes, she'd done the right thing.

# IV
## San Francisco

# 27

San Francisco had always been a city of delights for Elizabeth. Her mother used to take her there on shopping sprees, through one extravagant store after another, followed by a matinée or ballet performance, and always the ice cream soda at Blum's before starting home again. Other times her father would take the whole family for a day of joy — a visit to the zoo or a ride on the cable cars. The city always sparkled, the sun throwing strong lights and sharp shadows. If it rained, they simply went into one of the many warm and cozy places. Whatever the season, the city always had the tinge of a magical place.

But when Elizabeth got off the bus, she felt only a gray heaviness in the station, a Monday morning gloom, and a hopelessness in the people who dragged past her. Outside the streets seemed never to have been swept, a gust of wind chilled her, and she wondered where the joys of the city had gone.

"I'll be all right once I get to Maija's," she promised herself, and then, impatient to be there, she found a taxi. The address that Maija had given her was for a small street Maija said was in North Beach, not too far from the station, but the taxi took what seemed an endless detour and stopped at the top of a hill. The street plunged down perilously, and Elizabeth caught a glimpse of the dull green Bay, and the Bay Bridge in the distance.

"But this isn't the right street," she complained.

"What you want is down there, that very tiny street on the left. Can't drive into it. You'll have to walk from here. Four-twenty, please."

"Four-twenty! For this little ride! And I have to drag my suitcase all the way?"

"Sorry, girlie. The streets are torn. Have to take detours."

She gave him a five-dollar bill which he stuffed into his pocket and as she waited for the change, he shoved his hand deeper in his pocket as though looking for it, meanwhile suggesting by his expression that she was gravely at fault. She stood there, torn between anger at having been taken advantage of and disgust with herself for being as petty as he. Hardly an auspicious beginning.

"For heaven's sake, keep it," she said, deciding to finish the matter and chalk it up to experience. He offered no thanks. All right, I won't make this mistake again, she promised herself. Picking up her bags she comforted herself that within a few minutes she would be seeing Maija.

The alley in which the pale houses clustered together was narrow and gave the impression of a street that had been tucked in like an afterthought. She found the right place and rang the bell, although the name above it was Miles Dean. The buzzer sounded and she dragged her things up the four flights, expecting to find Maija.

She knocked at the door, but inside the din of a baby crying, another shouting at the top of his lungs, and a click-clack noise she didn't recognize, must have drowned out her feeble knock. She tried again.

"Come in!" someone roared.

Two small identical children, one of them completely naked, looked up at her. A man of about thirty-five with a full black moustache was working at a loom that spread across the middle of the living room floor. At last he looked up. "Yes, can I do something for you?"

"I'm looking for Maija Hrdlka. She gave me this address."

The man stood up and his face brightened at the sound of the name.

"You know Maija, do you? Tell me, do I know *you*?"

"I don't think so. Is Maija here?"

"How wonderful that you know her! How is she anyway? And where did you two meet? Are you a weaver?"

Then, as he felt Elizabeth's anxiety, he added quickly. "But she's not here, you know. We're just an address. Wait, I'll tell you where she lives."

Disappointed, Elizabeth waited while he looked through a desk so littered with sketches and bills, she didn't know how he could ever find anything. The room was in complete disarray, a clutter of toys, over-filled ashtrays, an Irish setter that unexpectedly rose from a corner and strode across the room, making it look even smaller. And yet the red and purple fabric on the loom was exquisitely ordered in a pattern of precise triangles and circles.

"I'll find it, just a minute. Will you stay for lunch? Cynthia, put another cup of water in the soup," he bellowed.

A small young woman with dank strands of hair across her face appeared at the kitchen door and stared.

130

She held a baby on one hip and was obviously pregnant with another. Unsmiling she looked Elizabeth up and down, then went back to the kitchen, shutting the door. Elizabeth shivered at her obvious antagonism, but felt worse when she saw what it did to Miles, who seemed shorter and older than before. Why do people do this to each other, she wondered, suffering for them both.

"Thanks for asking me, but I'll probably be having lunch with Maija," Elizabeth said, hoping to ease his embarrassment.

"Perhaps you'd like to see one of Maija's woven sculptures?"

She nodded, and he opened the sliding doors that led to a dining room criss-crossed with clothes lines heavy with wet diapers. Apologizing as he pushed them aside, he led her to a hall where a tall figure, woven in layer upon layer of lacy white fibers, stood in silent dignity. The figure suggested an airy softness, yet when she felt it, her fingertips were surprised at its firmness. The irritations of the morning passed; she was seeing Maija again, feeling her in this woven sculpture. She turned to Miles.

"It's very beautiful. If you have her address, I'd like to find her . . ."

"Oh sure," he said going back to the desk where he finally found the address. He spoke in a low voice, not wanting his wife to overhear, Elizabeth suspected. "Maija is a magnificent person, and a significant artist. You just wait and see. If I had it all to do over again . . ."

He stopped with a sigh, gave her the address, and offered to help her with the bags to the bus, that is, unless she preferred a taxi.

"The bus, although I don't know which one to take."

Cynthia's voice rasped from the kitchen door. "Miles, that work is due on Wednesday. You'll never get it finished."

"I'm just going to help the young lady, show her the bus stop," he called apologetically. The kitchen door slammed. A child wailed. One of the twins had been draping Miles' legs with yarn, but he patiently freed himself, and picking up Elizabeth's bags, led the way downstairs.

He waited with her at the bus stop. The wind had turned cold and they smiled as they caught each other shivering.

"You're a nice girl. What are you doing in a city like this? Looking for Maija, that's all right. But look, dear, be careful. This city has its dark side. I don't know much about you, but maybe you ought to go back to your nice home."

"I can't. There isn't any nice home," she said.

He helped her on the bus with her bags. "You've been today's gift to me. Live in peace," he said.

Impulsively she reached over and kissed him on the cheek. The busman shouted, "Let's *go!*" and she was on her way once more.

# 28

The house where Maija lived must have been at one time highly respectable, typical of the old Victorian homes with square bay windows and a fringe of fretted woodwork around the porch. Now the white and yellow paint peeled here and there and the wood flutings were chipped.

"So this is where I'll live," Elizabeth thought with a kind of excitement, as she climbed the narrow flights of stairs to the fourth floor. The vague possibility that Maija might not invite her to stay passed through her mind, but she knew, without doubt, that Maija was waiting for her.

Of the two doors that opened on the hall, Maija's was recognizable by the long bell pull of intricately braided jute from which hung a dozen small brass bells. Elizabeth tugged it and the bells tinkled, but it was the door on the other side of the hall that opened, releasing a chorus of dog noises. A woman at least sixty, small, with a mass of black dyed hair piled on top of her head, stepped into the hall. In her arms she cuddled a white poodle with red rheumy eyes.

"Were you looking for me, dear? Did you bring your doggie? I have an opening. I can take him now, if you like."

Elizabeth stared. Was the woman crazy? She stood there grinning at Elizabeth, her dark eyes taking her in from head to toe, while Elizabeth stared back at this amazing figure wearing a kimono, on which squirmed a red dragon, and incongruous pink-pommed carpet slippers. At last the woman, with a show of friendliness, understood.

"Oh, I'll bet you're lookin' for Maija. I was expectin' a customer and I thought you might be her. I groom dogs, mostly poodles. It's my profession. Maija ain't here, dear. She works afternoons down at the laundry. The Launderette. But don't go lookin' for her there;

it's a dangerous place. She'll be home later, maybe quarter past nine, something like that."

"Oh, I see."

"You look so disappointed, sweetie. Look, dear, let me tell you. The time will pass. Oh how it will pass. When you're old, it flies, but when you're young, I know, it crawls. Why talk about it? If you want to, you can leave your bags with me; they'll be safe, nothing will happen. And you can take a nice walk. Down there is the Japanese Trade Center, lots of nice shops. And there's a movie. Or come back and stay with me. I'm Sophie Adamek. Call me Sophie."

"You are really very nice. Thanks, I'd like to leave my bags with you."

"Sure thing. And what is your name?"

She was about to give her full name when she remembered she had best be careful. But "Elizabeth" slipped out before she could stop it.

Before Sophie could ask any more questions, they were interrupted by a soprano bark and a soft foreign voice hushing it. "There, Gigi is coming to see you, isn't that nice? Your little friend, Gigi!" Sophie said to her red-eyed poodle. Another old lady, who resembled Sophie but who dressed in black, puffed up the stairs. Her hair was dyed a false, harsh red, and two spots of rouge made circles on her pale cheeks. She greeted Sophie in a babble of language Elizabeth could not identify. The women embraced; the dogs barked in high short yips and sniffed each other. Sophie broke away to help Elizabeth move her bags inside her door and invited her to stay, but Elizabeth said no thanks, not now, but perhaps some other time.

Walking down the stairs, Elizabeth passed a young

woman or girl — it was difficult to tell in the dim light of the hall — who pressed herself against the wall so that Elizabeth could pass. The girl swept her dark slanted eyes over Elizabeth and then dropped her gaze. Thick black matted hair hung on both sides of her head. The girl unsettled Elizabeth and filled her with a vague disquiet that oppressed her and made her wonder if she had done the right thing in coming to the city. Never before had it seemed so dismal.

"All you need to do when you feel blue, is find one good thing," was what her mother used to tell her long ago. "Sheer Pollyanna," Elizabeth said, as the words came back. Yet it took no more than a bowl of hot soup in a tiny Japanese restaurant to warm her and give her the courage to face the remaining hours. She wandered through the Japanese Trade Center, lingering in the bright shops and browsing in the handsome bookstore where a recording of a Japanese koto sent its sparkling sounds flying like flashes of color through the gray day. Feeling she had stayed there too long, Elizabeth left, walked up one block and down another, noted the Japanese calligraphy on the street signs, admired an empty lot turned into a park that was a Japanese garden, and found a church that looked like a dingy Venetian palace with tracery windows and pigeons roosting everywhere. How incongruous it all was, she thought, the Victorian houses, the slick modern shops, a pair of brilliant paper carp hanging from a sign, a prim upright Methodist church with spanking white paint, and a paper stand that sold garish paperbacks nestled between a pungent fish store and a sedate shoji shop that displayed ancient samurai swords in the window. Yet San Francisco was like that, all mixed up.

Somehow it worked. The streets where she had walked seemed to form a natural village within the city.

Yet when she wandered beyond the borders, the charm disappeared as rubble-strewn lots bordered on vacant houses that stared blindly over the wasteland. Elizabeth shivered, then walked back rapidly to Maija's house, now a safe refuge. Using her coat as a blanket, she sat on the floor next to the hall window and watched the people on the street below. Nine o'clock was still far away.

She noticed an old woman waiting at a bus stop. Elizabeth was at the point of dozing off when she heard a cry as a car rushed up and stopped with a screech of brakes. A young man dashed out, snatched the old woman's purse, and knocked her over when she tried to fight for it. The woman lay sprawled out on the sidewalk, obviously stunned, as the car sped away with a nasty roar.

"Oh no! How could he do such a thing!" Elizabeth stood up, her heart beating furiously in shock and outrage. At that moment Sophie came out into the hall. Elizabeth, pointing below, explained what she had just seen and asked what they could do. Sophie didn't seem at all surprised; she went over to the window to see the woman picking herself up and tottering off down the street.

"Poor thing," Sophie said, "but it happens all the time in this city. This is a terrible city; the things that happen here! Poor girl, it's a shock for you. You come from a *nice* home. Tell me, what are you doing here? You're running away?" She sighed. "You're too young. So young. Do you want to wait in my apartment for Maija? No? Then let me bring you a blanket. That's a new coat, mustn't get it dirty."

"You're very nice to me. I appreciate it," Elizabeth said as she accepted the blanket. Alone once more, she curled upon the floor and thought: had it been only that morning that she had sat in her mother's sun-filled breakfast room over coffee? If so, what was she doing here? "I don't know," she moaned, suddenly uncertain. Soon afterwards she fell asleep.

She didn't know how long she slept, but a tickling feeling on her cheek and gentle stroking on her hair woke her, and she opened her eyes to see a small boy with velvety dark eyes bending over her.

"Hello," she said, sitting up.

"Nicholas? Nicki Nicholas?" a male voice called. A small young man with wavy dark hair, a long nose and eyes that showed clearly he was Nicholas's father, ran up the stairs. "Did he wake you? I told him not to. Nicholas, tell the lady you're sorry."

"That's all right. I was only waiting," she said.

"I live downstairs in 3-B, with Boris and Pete," the little boy said, pronouncing the words very carefully while his father — was it Boris or Pete? — stood by, obviously proud. Whoever they were, Boris and Pete, they loved this little boy. One could always tell the loved children, Elizabeth thought.

"Come, Nicholas, we mustn't bother the young lady," the father said, his manner also precise and exacting. Nicholas lingered.

"I'm going to be this old," Nicholas said, holding out five fingers, "and I want you to come to my party."

"Thank you. When will that be?"

"April nineteenth."

"But you've just had your birthday."

"I'll have another one, silly. Next April. You can come."

"Thank you. I'd love to," she said.

"And if it's like the last one, it will be wild," the father said, taking Nicholas's hand.

"Do you want some cookies with wheat germs? I helped make them," Nicholas said.

Elizabeth smiled. The father nodded at her, picked up Nicholas, and took him downstairs. Elizabeth heard a snatch of music drift up the stairs as the father and son entered their apartment.

Perhaps it wasn't such a bad city after all. Wasn't Nicholas a good omen? Sophie brought Elizabeth a pot of hot tea. Ten minutes later an enormous man walked up from below and gave her a plate of cookies.

"I'm Pete," he said in a quiet voice, "and these are from Nicholas."

"How nice! You're so kind, and so is he. Please thank him, and I thank you."

"If you want to stay with us until Maija gets home, you're welcome."

"Thanks anyway . . ."

Night came on and she had no idea what time it was. A million what-if's assailed her. What if she'd gone somewhere else, what if someone else were living with Maija, what if Maija didn't want her after all. . . . "I'm beginning to sound like a worried kid," she thought. She curled up in the blanket, looked out to the darkening sky with concern, then fell asleep again.

In her sleep she felt a cool hand stroking her forehead and hair. Someone was calling her name gently. She stirred and woke slowly, her neck stiff. As she turned, she opened her eyes and then sprang to life.

"*Maija!*"

"I knew you'd come," Maija said. "I've been waiting."

And as Elizabeth watched her unlocking the door, so straight and strong with the familiar ivory cap on her head and the black hair brushing against her face, tears streamed down her face. It was the end of a long day and she was so happy to be home at last. With Maija.

# 29

Much as she wanted to collapse once they entered the apartment, Elizabeth could not help but be stunned by the upright loom which extended diagonally from one corner of the whitewashed living room to the far corner of the next room. The vertical lines of the warp, white cotton string, seemed to shimmer in the dim light. The beginning of a tapestry in brilliant reds, yellows and magenta wools stretched unevenly across the bottom of the loom, the ends of the wool dangling from wooden pegs. At the far end of the loom a small table held an array of large spools, red, purple, orange, black . . . a burning center of color in the bare room.

"This is fantastic," Elizabeth said. "This is the tapestry you told me about?"

"No, this is another one. The first one fell through. But I can't talk about it now. I have to look at you to believe you're really here. I used to pretend you were here, and now, here you are!"

The girls stood apart studying each other. How lovely she is, Elizabeth thought, as if she were seeing Maija differently now than she had on the road, where she had only felt her strength. The square shoulders were still there and the straight posture. She's really beautiful, Elizabeth thought, beautiful to me anyway.

"Someday I shall do a tapestry of you, a portrait," Maija said, "and I'll call it North Star. A virgin column, all pale wools and silks, long streaming tussah silk for the hair. What do you think?"

Elizabeth blushed. "I wish I could do something for you. I'm so useless; can't do a thing, even if I wanted to."

"You can stay here with me. That's enough. It makes me happy to have you."

She held out her hand and led Elizabeth through the tiny apartment. The small kitchen was crammed with baskets, bowls, pottery, tiles — too much to take in at once — and then the bedroom, bare as a nun's cell, with a narrow white bed over which was a small tapestry, white with black letters spelling *Maru*. Later Elizabeth would find out what it meant, but now there was no time.

"Look," said Maija, "why don't I ask Sophie if I can borrow a bed for you. I think she has an extra one we can use."

It was a relief to be busy tugging it back into the room while Maija looked through a closet for fresh linens. She promised she would find a perfect spread for her, a Mexican pink and orange spread. Would Elizabeth like that?

The small talk over, the girls sat on the bed. There was so much to say, they could say nothing. Eventually Elizabeth spilled out the story of Sacramento.

"Was it all right for me to come here?" she asked. "I just couldn't go back to Nebraska. And I couldn't stay with my mother."

"You know, you have to make decisions, and you can't ever know what might have happened if you'd done some other thing. So you have to pick up the place where you are and go from there."

"That's a comforting thing to say. But I don't know where I'm going or what will happen. I wanted to see you, Maija. I couldn't think beyond that. Except for one vague idea. Promise you won't laugh."

"Well, what if I do? I might. Don't look so alarmed. What's your idea?"

"What I want to do, that is, if it's at all possible, if I'm not too entirely stupid . . . well, I'd like to do what you do. The tapestry or weaving, whatever it is."

"And why not? Liz, that's great. You can be my first student. My apprentice. How's that?"

"But I don't have very much money. And I should pay my share of food and rent."

"We can talk about that later. Let's say that I've just given you a scholarship. Hey, I like the sound of that. We don't have The Studio yet, the one I told you about, but we have our first student. Only there's one thing you should know even before we begin . . ."

"And that is what?" Elizabeth asked.

"It's not just manipulating threads and yarns. It's more than that. It's a whole way of living. It might not be what you think. It's work, sometimes hard work."

"But I can work. I can see things through, I think. It's the first time I've ever tried anything like this, so I'm a little nervous. But I want to. My fingers want to, you know?"

"That's the sign then, the good sign," Maija said.

They continued to look at each other and then Maija laughed. "There's so much to talk about and all I want to do is look at you. Tell me first, you must be hungry. Are you?"

"A little. But mostly, if it's possible and not too much trouble, I'd like to take a bath."

"Great, and I'll start supper in the meanwhile," Maija said, looking for a nightgown for Elizabeth while the water ran in the old-fashioned white bathtub that stood off the floor on claw-ball feet. Elizabeth was charmed with that and laughed at the nightdress, an enormous tent-like white flannel gown that Maija explained had been left behind at the Launderette.

Later, Elizabeth, flushed from the hot bath, sat in the kitchen while Maija finished stirring rice and vegetables in a pan over a hot fire. Elizabeth begged to do something. Maija asked her if she knew how to cook, because that would be her job as part of the scholarship.

"I can make stuffed mushrooms, caviar cream puffs and shrimp cocktail. Fudge too. My mother taught me."

"Great, we'll live on that!" Maija laughed. "You will think it a good exchange, won't you, the cooking for the weaving?"

"Maija, how can you even question that? I'd even scrub the floors."

"Then that's part of it too. You can scrub the floors. Only once in a while though," she was smiling — perhaps fooling, perhaps not.

Over rice and tea, Maija explained that the large commission she had come to San Francisco to work on had not worked out, but David Kazarian, the architect responsible, had found her a smaller commission, a tapestry for a new hospital entrance.

"It's not as big a job as the other, but it's a good one in its way. A beginning. But I have to work part-time. Promise not to laugh?"

142

"I might," Elizabeth said.

"That's all right. I'm managing a broken-down launderette and drycleaning place, a pathetic thing. The whole block has been torn down and our place will have to be vacated by the end of September. By that time the tapestry has to be done too. So, I'm hoping to get a teaching job somewhere. David knows of a few possible positions for me."

"So everything looks good for you."

"It does, for a fact. In the meanwhile in the back of my mind is The Studio. Elizabeth, it just has to happen. It's going to be unique, one of the most beautiful studios in the world. I'm not talking just about the setting and the physical part, which will of course be handsome, but about the spirit, the peacefulness, the vitality. A gem. And just think, you're the first scholarship student!"

"I'm really . . . well, I don't know what to say. It's more than I dreamed about. Oh Maija, I'm so happy!"

After dinner they cleaned the kitchen and went to bed. The narrow window showed a patch of dark sky pierced by a single star. Maija fell asleep in minutes but Elizabeth stayed awake. All through the night she heard the sounds of sirens and rushing cars. Police? Fire? Once she thought she heard gunshots, but it might have been the backfiring of a car.

She remembered what Miles Dean had said about the city. "Be careful. It has its dark side."

In the small hours of the morning she started with a shiver of fear, but when she stepped out of bed and watched Maija's even breathing, she felt calm and grateful that she was there with Maija; she returned to bed and eventually fell asleep.

# 30

The morning came in a gray bank of fog pressing against the narrow bedroom window, and when Elizabeth woke up, she missed the brilliant Sacramento morning sun. But only for a moment. The smell of coffee wafted through the apartment, and she stood at the door in the long nightgown, while Maija, in jeans and a sweater, made breakfast. The world became centered in the cozy little kitchen. She desired nothing more, to be no place else, to have no other companion.

"Maija, I'm so happy to be here. You cannot imagine what it means . . ." If only she could find the words to say what she felt, but Maija understood without words. Pouring honey from a glass jar into a smaller pot, she smiled easily in answer.

"How you sleep! It's the first day, so you have special dispensation. I'm making breakfast. But after this it's up to you."

"I'll have to learn how. But I will. I promise. Isn't it late? Don't you have to be at work?"

"No, the beauty of my job is that it doesn't begin until one, so I can do my own work mornings. And on Saturday, which is today, in case you didn't remember, I get out at six. So let's celebrate. How will you have your egg this morning?"

"I don't think I'm that hungry, Maija. The coffee smells wonderful."

"That's a treat too. And so is the fruit. And so is the long talk we'll have. Wait until you find out what a slave driver I am."

"I can just about see you with your whip," Elizabeth said, sitting down at the small table by the window. She could barely make out the tops of the houses on the next block and a round cupola dim and far away.

"I've been wondering about a few things," Maija said, as she circled her spoon around a segment of grapefruit, neatly and surely. Everything she did, she did decisively and perfectly, Elizabeth thought. In contrast, she thought herself careless and undisciplined. "Does anyone know you're in San Francisco or that you're with me? Both your father and mother may be very upset that you're missing, and they may be searching pretty intensively. Possibly here. San Francisco is a natural place for kids to go when they've left home."

"I didn't mention I'd be coming here because I didn't know myself until the last minute. And I didn't talk about you, Maija. I thought I would at first, but they were so full of their own problems, and they wouldn't understand anyway. So maybe it's just as well."

"They might make a lucky guess. We'll have to check the papers. Tell me, does anyone at all know you're here?"

"I didn't tell anyone my last name, nobody at all. I met Miles Dean, when I went to find you. And Mrs. Adamek. And Boris and Peter and Nicholas; but I don't think they even know my name. That's all."

"Not bad. Boris and Pete won't tell; they've been hassled by the police too long to go to them for any reason at all. Sophie will keep her mouth shut too. For one thing she's kind, and for another she's practicing without a commercial license. By the way, that's in strict confidence. I hope they don't put your picture in the paper and offer a reward . . ."

"I still have the black wig. I could be Wanda Byrd, I suppose." Elizabeth was joking, but Maija took her seriously.

"Not a bad idea. Only it will have to be Elizabeth, because Sophie knows you're Elizabeth. When you go out for your walks, be sure to wear the wig. Do you want to be Elizabeth Bird?"

"Sure. My walks?"

Maija grinned, looked down at her plate and then at Elizabeth with some amusement. "As a student at The Studio, you will be expected to live in accordance with the dignity of your work. Ahem! So I've thought up a schedule. In the morning we work together until lunch. I go to my job while you solve problems I've given you and do some reading I'll assign. Then at about three o'clock you'll have to go out to keep from becoming stir crazy; you'll take a walk for about an hour and a half during which time you'll meditate, observe life, pick up groceries and run errands if necessary. Sometimes we run out of yarns or paper. At six we'll each have a small snack, a bowl of soup or salad or whatever, and when I come home at nine, we can have the rest of our dinner, and maybe go out somewhere, or visit friends for awhile. On Sundays we're unscheduled, but there'll be exhibitions to see, trips to the country, long hikes, friends to visit, any number of things."

Elizabeth's voice was doubtful. "It sounds terribly organized."

"We can be flexible if we have to, or if it doesn't work out. But remember, art isn't just a matter of something

146

you do when you feel like it. It takes discipline. Don't look so worried. You'll even get to like it."

Elizabeth looked unconvinced. To change the subject, she asked about the girl she had met on the stairs.

"Oh," Maija shook her head as though thinking of something sad. "That must be Dora Rainwater. She's an Indian but I don't know what tribe. I can't get two words out of her, nor can anyone else. She's living in a room she rents from a couple downstairs, and she's waiting for her husband or boyfriend or someone who's in San Quentin. I've asked her to dinner, to tea. No use. She must be the loneliest person I've ever seen."

The mention of Dora quieted them, and they sat silently. Outside the fog blew, separated, thickened and moved away while fresh patches came to press up against the window.

"Want to see *The Phoenix?*" Maija asked.

They walked into the other room, and Maija sat back on her hard wooden stool while Elizabeth passed her fingers over the sensitive warp and touched the woven parts, marveling at the big bold structures that contrasted so easily with the tiny, delicate, airy textures.

"Do you know what a phoenix is?" Maija asked, and when Elizabeth said no, feeling humble and ignorant, Maija explained. "It's a very ancient mythical bird, probably a bird of good fortune, certainly a beautiful creature. It lives for five or six hundred years, burns itself on a funeral pyre, and then rises again from the ashes in all the glory of its youth, to begin the cycle once more. So I chose that to be the symbol for the hospital, a sign of hope and rebirth. David liked it too."

"David?" Elizabeth asked and then remembered it was probably the David Kazarian Maija had mentioned

147

yesterday. "It's a perfect idea, Maija, really, so beautiful. Do you always start the tapestry from the bottom? And how do you know where to go? Isn't it difficult?"

"Let me get the cartoon for you. The cartoon isn't a funny paper cartoon but the drawing of what the finished tapestry will look like." Maija pulled a roll of paper from a closet in the hall and spread it out. It turned out to be an enormous drawing on butcher paper taped together. Maija tacked it to the wall so that Elizabeth could see the whole design at once, neatly penciled, the colors indicated by numbers with pieces of yarn taped to the different sections. Elizabeth had to step back to see the drawing, it was that large. Now she had more of an idea of what it would look like.

But when she looked at Maija, her face was pale. "It's no use, Maija. I could never do anything like that. It's way beyond me. I don't know what I'm doing here. I can't even draw a straight line."

"Sure you can," Maija said, "You put down a ruler and draw a pencil against it. Liz, you're not really afraid of this, are you?"

"Yes, I am."

"Hmm. Look, that's your workbench over there. Sit down. We'll have the first lesson, a lecture. Ready? All right.

"Fear is the first and biggest enemy. You're *afraid* you can't draw a line, you're *afraid* you can't make a picture, you're *afraid* everything looks too complicated. You waste your life in fear, you fritter away all your good energy and intelligence. So first ask yourself, if you do fail, what do you really have to lose? And then ask yourself, what do you have to gain? Weigh the possibilities. I'll wait and when you're ready, I'll go on."

148

She *is* strange, Elizabeth thought, but she asked herself those very questions and soon she felt less panicky.

"Of course nobody would expect you to do in the beginning what has taken me a lifetime to learn. So why expect it of yourself? In time you will find your own way. Did you see the tapestry over my bed?"

"*Maru?*" Yes, I don't understand. I was going to ask you about it."

"It's a Japanese word meaning round or circle. You'll see it written on ships. But words have different meanings. One day I read somewhere, I can't recall where, that *Maru* has another meaning; it means love for the work you do, total devotion to your craft; it means doing it every day the best way you know how, giving it the best of your energy. I don't know any other word that says so well what my whole life means or how I feel about my work."

"That's amazing," Elizabeth said softly, deeply impressed, and feeling less certain of herself than ever.

"I tried to find out more about the word in dictionaries, and I asked my Japanese friends, but they didn't know. So it may not be correct, but that one word says it all for me. Oh Liz, don't look so serious. Or doubtful. You'll someday understand it, that's all. Come. End of lecture. Let's work!"

Twenty minutes later Elizabeth sat before her loom, a simple construction of wood two by three feet. "I had that one, but next time you will make your own," Maija warned. She talked a little about looms and wanted to explain about warps and why some were better than others. She opened a quiet flax curtain in the living room that Elizabeth had not even noticed, uncovering a vast array of yarns wound on spools or hanging down in skeins. So much color all at once made Elizabeth gasp and laugh.

"I wouldn't have dreamed this was here. All your walls are so bare. And this is blazing."

Maija picked up spools of carpet warp, seining cord and linen, making Elizabeth feel them and stretch them and learn their differences.

"You know so much. How will I ever remember it all?" she sighed.

"You will. Touch it over and over again until your fingers know the difference."

And so that morning Elizabeth put her first warp on the small loom. She was ready to begin her first sampler when Maija shrieked that she was due at work in ten minutes. After a wild scurry, during which Elizabeth found an apple and cheese slices for Maija's lunch, Maija left and Elizabeth was once more alone.

# 31

She stood at the window watching Maija rush down the street, varying her walk with an occasional skip like a child in a hurry to go somewhere yet too dignified to run.

"I never realized how wonderful you were," Elizabeth whispered to the figure disappearing down the street. On the trip Maija had been so much the leader and guide on whom Elizabeth had leaned that she had thought of her only as a means of reaching home safely.

Now, ashamed that she hadn't recognized what kind of person Maija really was, she thought to herself how amazing it all was that she should be here and that this angel — for an angel could have done no more — was here to take care of her once more.

The room took on a lonely silence. Elizabeth walked through the apartment, haunted by it. She stopped to examine more closely all the objects in the kitchen, the baskets hanging from hooks, the posters on the outsides of the cabinets and on a large cork board, a treasury of things. Surely these would tell something about Maija. Announcements of weaving and painting exhibitions, two of them in France, two in San Francisco and one in Switzerland; postcards with scrawled messages on the back; announcements of coming shows; stapled in one corner a listing of prices from a health food store. And all around were reproductions of tapestries, clipped from magazines, postcards and announcements. Elizabeth looked at one already framed: The Lady with the Unicorn; she loved it immediately and looked at it for a long time, the pink-rose background and the tall calm lady sitting among the flowers. In contrast, a photograph of what must have been a huge orange-yellow tapestry that looked like elephant ears with slits, and in a deliberate hand at the bottom, "With love to Maija . . ." and a signature she could not read. A detail from an ancient Peruvian weaving, a large black bird that looked like sculpture but was woven, and an actual small tapestry done with the finest black and white yarns, showing birds sitting in a tree.

Open as Maija was, appearing to hold back nothing, she emerged for Elizabeth as someone mysterious, someone yet to be known.

Elizabeth went to the bedroom, noticed the wicker chest at the foot of Maija's bed, and wondered idly if she should look through it. Her hand was on the lock, but then she pulled it away, disgusted with herself. Maija was more than generous, and here she was, already breaking trust. The word *Maru* looked down at her.

"It's so quiet," she said, surprised to hear her own small voice. She sat on the bed and waited. So much of her life was spent in waiting. When she was small, how many times her mother had kissed her goodbye before an afternoon rehearsal. Half-apologizing for leaving her alone, her mother would promise to come back soon, and Elizabeth would stay behind and watch after her little brother. Now, as she sat on Maija's bed, she remembered the fragrance of her mother's perfume as she bent over to kiss her and the way Elizabeth had wanted to cling to her and cry, "Don't go, Mama!" But she hadn't cried. She had learned to wait the long hours.

"As if Maija were my mother," she said, analyzing the comparison. But in a way hadn't Maija taken her mother's place? "No, that's not it at all," she protested, and then looking at *Maru* once more, she went back to the loom.

Weaving wasn't as easy as it looked. First, she had to remember to lift the warps with her left hand and slip the bobbin through, but it seemed more natural to point the bobbin, which Maija said was wrong. She struggled with that, then discovered that her yarn was drawn too tight and she had to rip it out. Yet when she did it again, purposely leaving it loose, uneven loops bulged at the sides.

Maija had said, "You mustn't worry. In a few days it will all come naturally to you and your fingers themselves will be sensitive enough to know what is going on."

Determined to surprise Maija, she put in her weft, pulled it out, and tried again until it felt even, with a good tension. Her first sampler, to be done only in black and white, was a challenge of sorts. She was on the verge of trying out a series of block-like forms, hoping to surprise Maija by going on ahead, but she forgot how to tie off the yarn. She tried it one way, then another, and finally, with a mild "Damn," decided to let it go. If it weren't right, she'd only have to rip it out again.

Almost four o'clock. She found herself chilled and the air outside too gray to be inviting. Time passed so slowly when you were alone, she thought. Then she snapped her fingers. She still had her backpack at Sophie's. She would go and get it with a perfectly legitimate excuse for visiting.

She knocked at Sophie's door, which opened a crack to reveal one bright eye looking out. Then the door flung open wide, a greeting for a friend. Immediately a chorus of barks filled the air.

"Shah! Hush! Shhhhhh! Stop it, Fritzie, stop, Marcel! Be good doggies now, this is Elizabeth, our friend," Sophie admonished two elderly but beautifully groomed black poodles, both decorated with rhinestone collars and blue ribbons, as they pranced around Elizabeth.

"This one here on the table is Elizabeth Taylor!" Sophie said, proudly pointing to still another ancient poodle with thinning hair who waited for her grooming. The dog sighed asthmatically, like a tired old actress.

"And Elizabeth Taylor's mother, Mrs. Marzak. Mrs. Marzak, this is Maija's new friend I told you about."

Mrs. Marzak, a tiny, erect lady, was even more ancient than her dog. Dressed in a black coat with a fur collar eaten with age and wearing a hat of crushed maroon velvet, she perched on the edge of her chair and held a glass of hot tea in her hand. She nodded formally at Elizabeth.

Where, Elizabeth wondered, did all these old ladies come from? Their lives seemed as mysterious to her as Maija's.

"How about a cup of tea, my dear? Or a glass of tea? Which do you like?"

"Whichever it is," Mrs. Marzak said, "for a chilly afternoon is nothing better."

"Thank you. I'll try it in a glass," Elizabeth said, grateful for their company and glad that her decision seemed to please Sophie. While she waited, she looked around the crowded living room; everywhere pictures, paintings and photographs of dogs covered the tables and walls. The was one gentleman who could have been Mr. Adamek, and over the fireplace hung an icon, a religious picture painted on wood, primitive as a peasant painting.

Mrs. Adamek returned with the tea, and while Elizabeth sipped it — finding the glass very hot and wondering why anyone would choose to drink tea this way — the two women broke into a spirited conversation in a foreign language which Elizabeth could not place. She found herself growing embarrassed as they looked at her and obviously discussed her. Soon Sophie explained.

"We are saying only in Yugoslavian, that you are a beautiful young girl. Now is best time of your life."

"Thank you," she said and then wondered what she should say. It would hardly do to tell them that it must

154

be nice to be old, because she really thought being old must be the worst thing imaginable. They smiled, but under their smiles she sensed lifetimes of disappointment; that was how old people were. Yet these ladies were so dear, and she was suddenly touched by them, by their concern for the wheezing Elizabeth Taylor and the handsome elderly Fritzie and Marcel.

When it was time for Elizabeth to go, Sophie, neither as old nor delicate as Mrs. Marzak, gave her the backpack and a copy of the *San Francisco Chronicle*.

"I thought maybe because you are in the city now, you would enjoy looking at it. It's interesting," she said, her eyes suggesting it would be wise for Elizabeth to look at it.

"Thanks so much," Elizabeth said, and then patting the poodles and even kissing Elizabeth Taylor, she took her knapsack and the paper and left. Her apartment was more quiet than ever, and in the silence she thought she knew why ladies got together every day for tea.

Elizabeth turned on the light, put the newspaper on the floor, and then, as she had always done before, kneeled on the floor to read it. She turned the pages slowly, picking up a headline here and there. And then she stopped short.

On one of the inside pages was a small box with a familiar picture, the one she had taken for her yearbook, with Elizabeth van Vliet written in black type below it. The large gray eyes looked out from the three-quarter view, and the giveaway hair fell smoothly down on either side of her head. A short article explained that her parents were frantically searching for her, and a reward of $500 would be given to anyone who knew where she was.

Had her mother put in the ad or her father or possibly

both? So they were worried, they missed her. If only she could call them.

As if that were not enough, the classified ads held a message for her under *Personal.*

*Elizabeth, please call. We love you*
*and want you. Dad.*

Tears burned her eyes. Her father must have been terribly worried to have permitted himself to write such an emotional appeal.

"I'll have to call them," she said. "I can't let them go on worrying." That was all there was to it.

"But if I do then they'll make me tell them where I am. I know it; and I'll have to go home!"

Her eyes wandered to *The Phoenix* on the loom. The flames and ashes were scarcely complete, yet she could see the sketch on the wall behind and the drawing of the proud bird. Her own loom, strung for the first time that morning, rested beside Maija's large loom. She had already begun her first weaving.

"I'll call him. I really will," she promised out loud to nobody in particular. "But not now, later."

# 32

Within a week Elizabeth van Vliet retreated into a dim shadow and Elizabeth Bird emerged. Change your name and you change your person. Wanda Byrd had been a wanderer; Elizabeth Bird was Maija's disciple. Stifling her yawns, she got up at six to prepare a break-fast of whole grains, which she told herself she liked, although she longed for her mother's blueberry muffins. She cut the heavy loaf of bread which Maija bought from a friend who was trying to get into the bakery business. Elizabeth put it down after the first slice — unimproved by honey — and was on the verge of asking Maija if they had to have it, when Maija beat her to the answer.

"Marnie puts everything in it, wheat germ, molasses, sprouted alfalfa and all that. If we don't like it, it's because we're spoiled and decadent."

I'd rather be spoiled in some ways, Elizabeth thought, but Maija could be stubborn about such things, so she kept quiet. Is marriage like this, she wondered.

As the mornings passed, Elizabeth had the feeling that she was in a convent. The silence which had at first unnerved her became a blessing, allowing her to listen to herself as she worked. Sometimes when they opened the window, the faraway noises from the street below or the sounds of Boris's hi-fi or a neighbor's arguing made noise around the edges, but within the studio a softness and clarity of silence was the rule.

Once Maija burst into song and then begged Elizabeth's pardon.

"I mustn't do this to you. I'm not a singer — don't know anything about music anyway. Let's see what you're doing."

She slipped off her stool to look at Elizabeth's work. What seemed perfect to Elizabeth revealed a hundred faults to Maija's eye. The finger pointed them out. "You didn't tie this off right, Liz, and the tension is still too tight. Here the curve is too abrupt."

"I knew it wasn't right, but I didn't want to interrupt you."

"Why not? That's what I'm here for."

"I didn't want you to think I was stupid."

"Who said you were stupid? But doing things wrong when you know they're wrong isn't exactly bright, is it? Liz, dear, I don't mind explaining, fifty times if it's necessary. Sooner or later your fingers will understand, and they'll remember forever. Fingers can be intelligent. Really, that's true. So let's rip it out back to there and begin again."

"But Maija, it took me all afternoon to do that much."

"Want me to rip it out for you if it's too much for you to bear?"

Elizabeth's look said no. "Can't I cut it with the scissors?"

"Sure. But be careful about cutting the warp."

"Everything is so dangerous! What if I cut the warp?"

"I'll teach you to mend it, but be careful and you won't cut it."

And so it went. Maija was a born teacher, understanding but strict, not given to complimenting her student. But one day after a long session when Liz had to redo a section of her sampler three times, Maija said, "Not bad. You'll be ready to begin your first tapestry soon."

"Really?" Elizabeth could hardly wait to begin an actual tapestry, but she did not ask. She was already learning to stay her patience.

All too often they forgot lunch until it was almost too late, and so they ate little. Maija, slipping on her jacket and taking a last swallow of tea, would spend the last minutes giving Elizabeth assignments in reading art history and design study.

"Maija, why can't I go to work with you?" she asked one day.

"I'll take you there someday. Not today."

"I'll surprise you. One day I'll bring you a beautiful sinful cream puff without the slightest trace of wheat germ, and you'll have to invite me in."

Maija stopped lacing her boot and became serious.

"Liz, you must never come down there. Promise me you won't. It's a terrible neighborhood. Knifings, gunfights, rapes and half the time no police at all. It's a jungle. No place for you."

"But I get lonesome."

"I'd rather be here too. But it won't be long. Next year I'll teach and maybe the year after that we'll have The Studio. But Liz, I mean it about your staying away from the Launderette. All right?"

"All right, I suppose."

Elizabeth finished packing Maija's six o'clock snack in a brown paper bag and gave it to her, looking into the strong gentle face.

"Be good now," Maija said. Like a mother, Elizabeth thought.

"I will," she promised. But she's not my mother at all, she said to herself. So why had she even thought of it?

"I'm good. I'm a good girl," Elizabeth said to herself. It sounded childish, yet for her it was a new state. She had never tried to be good in her life. Now she worked as soon as Maija left, worked on her frame loom until her neck and shoulders ached, determined to get through her "preliminary scales" as soon as possible. And she studied. Each week she and Maija went to the library and came home with four books each, to say nothing of the long texts she nibbled at, a chapter every two days.

"But by three-thirty you must clear out. Get some fresh air," Maija had said. "You must not jail yourself."

So Elizabeth put on the black wig with its shining bangs and long straight hair. Maija laughed and swore she looked half-oriental. But Elizabeth grew to like it. Sometimes on her long walks she would see the tall, slender black-haired girl reflected in a shop window and wonder if that were really she and if she were being metamorphosed.

At first Elizabeth spent her walking time wandering aimlessly, but within a few days she became aware of routes that she might follow, each of them taking in a different mood of the city and each of them offering treasures: the music store where she stopped to listen to records and flirted with the young man who let her play them; the small park where she helped children on the swings; the sophisticated shops on Union Street where she peered through the windows at antiques and Chinese baskets and new clothes; a Greek grocery where she bought black olives and feta cheese; and a Jewish bakery where she found herself sighing for the fragrant loaves of bread and wishing that Maija had never heard of Marnie's unbearable experiments.

Shopping for groceries was a new responsibility. Maija's eyes twinkled that first week as she gave Elizabeth an envelope full of bills. "That has to last us a week. See what you can do."

It seemed like so much money. Maija had suggested the small Japanese store around the corner. Though it looked dark and grimy, it was a good store and Mr. Hommada was helpful.

Helpful *and* pleasant! He smiled at the new customer as she shoved the cart through the aisles, picking up first a green pottery jar of soy sauce and then a six-sided canister of tea on which were painted children flying kites. Maija will be charmed, she thought. She found a package of seaweed, and Mr. Hommada himself pulled out a piece to show how each frail textured sheet was lovely to look at. Into the shopping basket went canned goods with their brilliant labels, mermaids, lotuses, dragons, imaginary flowers, an emperor and his empress, a butterfly blessing a stalk of bamboo. What was in the cans? She did not know and could hardly guess. "But they are beautiful," she thought, "and I can always do something with them." A lotus root, long white dikon radishes, twists of ginger roots, and finally seven tangerines. That done, she walked up to the counter where the genial Mr. Hommada totaled the purchases on a small adding machine. They came to two dollars more than the amount in the envelope.

"I'll have to put something back," she said apologetically, thinking they could do best without the soy sauce and the package of dried shrimps, transparent little fellows, each with tiny bright eyes.

The cool air outside brought Elizabeth to her senses. Too late she realized they needed butter, lettuce, soap, and look at the luxuries she'd bought! What should she do about it now?

As she entered the house she met Dora, and immediately, at the sight of the unsmiling girl, she forgot the problem. "Hello, Dora. My name is Liz, and I live upstairs. Would you like to come up and have some tea with me?"

Without acknowledging that she had been spoken to, Dora moved on, and Elizabeth, saddened, went upstairs. Looking over her purchases she decided that she'd have to make the best of it, that's all. The tangerines, carefully placed on a wooden board, were lovely to look at. But what about eating? The can with the exotic mermaid, when opened, held a reddish pickled fish that smelled vile. She had paid eighty-nine cents for that? "How could I?" she asked herself. She consoled herself that at least they had rice, and she set the table so that it looked appetizing.

When Maija came in, Elizabeth confessed. "I've done a terrible thing."

Maija looked over the purchases, then laughed. Seeing that Liz was upset, she put her arm around her. "It's all right, honey. You're just getting educated all at once. You might even develop a taste for this kind of food. Don't worry. We'll live through it."

"How good you are, Maija!" Elizabeth said. And then as she put the detestable fish in the pan to heat it, she thought of something. "Now I know why Mr. Hommada smiles so much!"

# 33

One week passed. Two weeks. Three. May slipped into June and June was promising to fly by.

"It makes me so happy to be with you," Elizabeth told Maija one Sunday morning. The day spread before them with all the wonder of a holiday. She was preparing a picnic lunch for the two them, since Maija wanted to look up something in a museum, and after that, they planned to walk along the shore. Later they would stop to visit a few of Maija's friends Elizabeth had met the night before at the bar where Maija liked to go on Saturday nights because of the accordion music there. Elizabeth found it slightly odd that Maija, such an austere person all week, could, without losing character, enjoy her beer and beat out the rhythms of the accordionist. That Maija should have any quirks at all made her all the more human and lovable.

"I just wish that this life of ours would never end. Never. It's perfect," Elizabeth said, biting into an apple. "See, even the Lady and the Unicorn are happy for us. Their world is perfect and so is ours."

Elizabeth didn't notice that Maija's eyes had narrowed a little, as though she were thinking, and that she neither answered, nor smiled politely at Elizabeth's fantasy.

"What are you going to wear today?" Elizabeth joked mildly. "Your Cardin suit or the Nina Ricci? Shall we take the Rolls or the Mercedes?"

"Let's take the dogcart," Maija said, not always enjoying Elizabeth's childish humor. "But let's get going. We have a lot of ground to cover."

But even a slight impatience failed to deter Elizabeth. She loved Maija; Maija was her teacher, her mother, her friend, the only person she needed. Maija could neither say nor do anything wrong.

The following Wednesday, as Elizabeth was finishing a set of designs on paper, Maija walked in, a dress box under her arm.

"What's this all about? It's only three o'clock," Elizabeth said.

"Well, I'm taking the afternoon off," Maija said. "I'm going out tonight."

"Really? Where are we going? And can you get someone to substitute for you at the Launderette?"

"First question. I'm afraid it's not 'we,' Liz, because this is something I'm doing alone. And yes, on occasion I can find someone to take my place."

"But where are you going? I don't understand."

"Right now, Liz, I want to sleep for an hour. Where's the alarm clock? Okay. One hour," she said, turning the hands. "You don't mind if I nap, do you?"

"Of course not." Elizabeth looked puzzled as Maija closed the door of the bedroom. She went back to her designs, wondering if perhaps Maija would have a surprise for her. Maybe that's why she was being so mysterious.

At four exactly the alarm went off, and Maija ran a long hot bath for herself.

"I wish I had some bath oil for you," Elizabeth said. "I love long hot baths more than anything. Can I get you a cup of tea, Maija?"

"That would be awfully nice, Liz. Thanks very much."

Elizabeth brought the cup on a tray to Maija soaking in the tub. As she stood above her, holding her own cup of steaming tea, Elizabeth looked down and thought how lovely Maija looked with her neat olive-skinned body shimmering under the water and her thick black hair spreading out above it.

"How are you going to get your hair dry?" Liz asked.

"It will dry. Anyway, you won't believe it, but I do have a small dryer."

"It's hard to believe *you* would have something like that. Where are you going?"

"Somewhere," Maija said dreamily looking away from Elizabeth. Elizabeth looked at her, hurt; Maija didn't want to tell her. Didn't she trust her? Hurt was like a bruise, but Maija did not seem to notice.

"And Liz, I'm sorry that you'll have to have dinner without me tonight. I won't be home, most likely until tomorrow morning sometime. Think you can manage? I'm sure you can."

"Oh sure, sure," Elizabeth said, taking Maija's empty teacup back to the kitchen. "Want me to rub you down with the towel? Want a massage? I'm not too bad. Want me to do your hair?" she asked, feeling like a puppy jumping for a bone.

Maija smiled her refusal. Elizabeth sat on the bed and watched her dress, pure white underwear, everything clean. A long slip. And from the box, a long jersey violet dress with low front and long sleeves, a scarlet chiffon scarf, precisely the right, if unexpected, color to flow around her neck; sandals woven with the finest purple suede, an exotic velvet evening bag she took from her chest at the foot of the bed, and a bracelet, a twist of heavy gold. She stood before the mirror making up her eyes.

Could it be Maija doing all this?

"That dress wasn't exactly left over at the Launderette, was it?" Elizabeth asked. Maija's closet was filled with oddities, clothes that were never claimed or odd gifts from friends.

"This is a gift from a friend," Maija said coolly and decisively.

When she was finally made up, dressed, and transformed into a creature so exotic that Elizabeth wondered if she were dreaming, Maija said, "I have a little time. Let's see your designs. How are they coming? Any problems?"

Elizabeth handed them to her and Maija studied them. Then putting them on the table she pointed out why this one worked and why the next one failed; the third was a good design but didn't solve the problem; and this next, what was this, something with possibilities but Elizabeth wasn't quite ready for it yet. This last design pleased Maija, nevertheless. But it would be best for Elizabeth to work further on the first design. Elizabeth looked less depressed. After all, Maija had not changed entirely. She was her teacher, believable once more, the genuine Maija still there under the violet gown and the eye make-up.

How Maija could have distinguished the horn of the car below from any other street noise, Elizabeth did not know, but a few minutes later she announced that she had to go. Pulling a dark wool evening cape from a back closet, she embraced Elizabeth quickly, and disappeared down the stairs. Standing at the window, Elizabeth looked down and saw her crossing the street to a long black sports car, where a tall man got out to greet her with a kiss. Then they got in the car and drove away.

The silence which Elizabeth had come to love now became oppressive. A disappointment, as childish as the feeling of not being invited to a party, clung to her. Why was she left home alone? That's not reasonable, she argued with herself. But who was that man? Where was Maija going?

An impulse told her to look in the news, so she borrowed the paper from Sophie. In the entertainment section, a column appeared about the opening of an important show in a museum in Palo Alto. That could account for it and for the earliness of their departure.

Tomorrow the opening would be reported in the Society column. She was content that that was probably it, but why hadn't Maija trusted her?

Out of long habit she looked through the Personal Ads. And there it was again, appearing as it had every day since she had left home, only the words were changed slightly from time to time.

*Elizabeth, come home or phone. We miss you and love you and want to help you. Dad*

She sat on her hard workbench and wondered if she should call, if she should go back. Her father loved her, that was certain. And Maija had left. But didn't Maija love her too? It was confusing. She sat there wondering what to do as the light outside dimmed and the silence grew even more oppressive.

A brisk knock on the door startled her out of her reverie. She jumped. Not so much frightened as careful, for Maija made her keep the door locked when she was home alone, Elizabeth called out, "Who is it?" and waited.

To her relief the familiar voice answered, "It's Boris, and we want to invite you to have dinner with us tonight."

"Oh Boris, how nice! How good it is to see you again!" she cried as she opened the door. She repressed an urge to throw her arms around him. That nice man who wanted to rescue her from an endless gloomy solitude . . . how did he know?

She recovered in a few seconds. "That's very welcome. What can I bring?"

"Yourself. Nicholas is so excited, he's jumping all

167

over. So I'm glad you're coming. In about ten minutes, or whenever?"

She decided to bathe, to put on fresh underwear, to find a long skirt her mother had bought for her when she was home, and a white shirt. There, she could dress-up too with a touch of eye make-up and a touch of fragrance.

Their apartment was a home, a true home, with a smattering of antiques, worn velvet easy chairs, ancient toys, a chess table and an excellent hi-fi on which Peter was playing a Mozart quartet. Fragrant odors wafted from the tiny kitchen. Nicholas demanded to be kissed and insisted that she look at his train set, an enchanting and aged representation of the Orient Express. Peter, really an enormous man, worked deftly on a geometrical piece of needle point as he beamed down on Nicholas, and Boris kept calling from the kitchen that it would be ready in a few minutes, that they must have a little more patience and that nothing in the world takes so much care as a soufflé.

As the evening passed, Elizabeth learned that Pete was a plumber and Boris, who sometimes taught night school, was a mathematician involved in writing an abstract, the pages of which were stacked neatly on a rolltop desk. Elizabeth was the admiring guest they needed. She praised the good music, showed she was enchanted with all their skills, played with their cat, and wondered how she could express the harmony and love she felt among them.

"Do you know," she asked after her second glass of wine, "that I love you people and I want to applaud you?" She put down her wine glass and clapped for them. "Good Lord, what kind of a nut am I?" she

168

asked herself. But they responded, the three of them applauding for her.

She could have stayed forever. But Peter put on a Mozart quintet . . . it was really a Mozart evening . . . and she felt the sadness come upon her again. It was the same recording that her father used to play in his loneliness in Lincoln.

She thanked them profusely and left. In the hallway she leaned back from the stairs, listened to the sad, tender music, and tears filled her eyes.

# 34

By ten the next morning Elizabeth had been at the loom for three hours, and still Maija had not appeared. Nervously threading the wools around the bobbins and working with fitful bouts of concentration on a huge sampler filled with design problems that Maija had given her, Elizabeth wondered what she should do. At what point should she tell someone, Sophie perhaps, that Maija wasn't home? She slumped on her bench disconsolately, a child abandoned by her mother.

"No, I'm an *adult*," she told herself. She still wished Maija were home. Sighing, she went back to work.

At ten-fifteen Maija quietly opened the door and came in, still in the evening dress she had worn the night before. The relief that flooded through Elizabeth must have been audible it was so great, and in the split second that she looked at Maija, Elizabeth noticed that she seemed tranquil, not unusually happy and yet not really sad. But after that one glance, Elizabeth returned to her loom, playing the insulted child whose mother has been away too long.

"Good morning, hello and all that," Maija said.

"Hello." A small chilly hello.

Maija walked over to Elizabeth and stood in back of her, as though it were an ordinary morning like any other. She pointed out a place where the yarn was pulled too tight and another area that needed a slight correction. "It's coming, Liz. It's a tough set of problems I've given you but these are excellent."

"And boring too, don't forget that, after three weeks," Elizabeth said accusingly, wanting to turn around and tell Maija how glad she was to have her back. What was this pride that wouldn't let her do it?

"Maybe you're right. Three weeks can be a drain. And you've already done all these."

Maija picked up the small pile of work Elizabeth had already finished — the first tapestry in black and white; a translation of a section of a photograph to tapestry form; and a problem in textures in which one yarn had to be used to create a one-color design. While Maija pondered these, Elizabeth plodded away on her new design problem, remaining aloof, almost unapproachable. Maija paid no attention to this childish reproof.

"Maybe it's time, Liz, for you to take off on your own. How would you like to make your own tapestry? You'll finish the design problem, of course. But in addition to that, you can design anything you like, use any colors, carry it out any way you like. You'll be absolutely free."

"Maija, you mean it? Really?"

The coolness vanished. She jumped up and threw

her arms around Maija. "Why did you stay away so long? Where did you go? Why didn't you tell me? I missed you."

"You survived, didn't you?" Maija said dryly. "I'll tell you when I'm ready. I thought you'd be pretty happy to do something on your own."

"Oh, I am, Maija. I've had millions of ideas. Can I use any of the yarns?"

"It's all up to you. Everything. And now I think I'd better change!"

Elizabeth put up a pot of hot water for tea, and in a short while Maija, back in the familiar jeans and a sweater, was picking up the bobbins and working once more on *The Phoenix*. "What did you do last night?" she asked Elizabeth casually.

Now it was Elizabeth's turn to smile mysteriously. "That's for you to find out," she said. Two could play this game as well as one. Maija laughed and returned to *The Phoenix*.

# 35

Since she had begun working with Maija, Elizabeth had visions of tapestries she would do as soon as she were free from the exercises which Maija had set for her. At times she felt that they were fences around her, and she couldn't wait to get out and do something of her own. Yet now that she was given total freedom, she couldn't imagine what she wanted to do.

"I'll choose the colors first," she thought, pulling back

the protective linen drape and letting the brilliant hues of the woolen yarns beam out at her. "Beam out" was the way she thought of colors now. Maija had given her a book on color to read, and now she thought she could see the wave lengths of color as they flowed; the reds and oranges in tight, high-pitched waves and the blues and purples in longer, more flowing vibrations. As for the earth colors, the natural black, never truly black, and the natural white, so much softer than the chemically dyed whites, had a subtlety that appealed to her more and more. She could never refrain from putting her fingers on them, as though they could speak to her. She was falling in love with wool and with color, and it pleased her, as though it were a sign that she was on the right path.

"But Maija, I don't know what to do. My brain is empty all of a sudden."

Maija at her own loom, pulling at the heddles and whirling the bobbins in and out while she hummed a vaguely audible tune, stopped to say, "Don't worry, it will come. You might do some drawings; use charcoal, or the felt pens. And if you work on your problem tapestry now and then and let your mind go blank where the new idea for the project is concerned, something may occur to you."

Later, after Elizabeth had used half a newsprint pad but still had not come up with anything, and the girls were having lunch, Maija went on, "This is something you mustn't be impatient about, or despondent. You have something to say, but it may be buried deep within you, like a bulb in the ground. Nature will work with you, if you let it happen, and the idea will come. I can't tell you more because it's different for everyone."

172

But Elizabeth was impatient. And when three o'clock came and she still had not come up with anything, she put on her black wig and coat and started down the stairs to take a walk. A slow dismal fog filled the air, penetrating everywhere; she shivered and then found herself almost bumping into Dora. She stepped back and apologized to the heavy, brown figure.

"Dora, I'm sorry. I didn't even see you. I was thinking about something else."

Dora stopped, looked into Elizabeth's face, and waited. Again, the misery of the girl acted like a magnet.

"I've got an idea, Dora. Won't you come for a walk with me? It gets awfully lonesome up there. I wish you'd come."

But Dora only shook her head and passed into the house. Elizabeth walked through the gray city, stopped in at Mr. Hommada's, and even there, the bright colors of the fruits and vegetable and fish seemed to glow only dully through the darkness.

What had happened to all the colors she loved so much? How could they have left her like that?

Nothing seemed to work, so she stayed with the tapestry of problems, growing more and more desperate. Maybe I don't have anything to say. What if it were all in vain? That she could become a good craftsman in time, she knew without fail; sooner or later it would happen. But to be an artist, to burst with ideas and forms and colors, like Maija, that was something else. If only she had *proof* that she could create — but then, was there such a thing as proof? She would talk it over with Maija that night, she decided, as she finished a perfectly executed circle on the loom.

That evening Maija did not come home until late. Elizabeth waited and wondered. When she did arrive, her face was deathly pale, and she seemed unable to talk. Elizabeth, frightened, helped her to bed where she lay breathing heavily while Elizabeth covered her with blankets to keep her from shivering.

"What's wrong? Shall I get a doctor?" Elizabeth asked.

Maija shook her head. "I'll be all right in a few seconds. There's nothing wrong with *me*. Get me some wine, and then I'll tell you."

Elizabeth hurried to get the wine, which Maija sipped slowly. Then, looking less pale, she got up to wash her face and brush her hair. Insisting that she didn't want to go to bed yet, she sat on a kitchen chair while Elizabeth fussed about her.

"You know I told you about the place where I work, near the vacant block? It's about the most sordid place I know. Anyway, someone heard a baby crying at one end of the lot, near an abandoned house. Two women in the shop went out to look, and sure enough there was the baby sitting there bawling; his mother, a young black woman, had been attacked, probably raped and certainly stabbed, and looking half-dead already. I've never seen anything so awful. That poor baby just couldn't understand; he was so afraid. Well, we called the police and they sent an ambulance, not too quickly either, and I kept the baby until someone who knew his grandmother went to get her so she could take him. That's why I was late."

"Will the mother live?" Elizabeth asked.

"Who knows? Maybe."

"You read about things like that. I can never quite

picture them; I can't believe people would really do things like that."

"Liz, my innocent. My innocent Liz. It happens. It happens again and again and again. And there's no sense to it. That's why I don't want you going there, ever. And yet, you know, there is such a sweetness about the people who come into the place, some of them, a kind of warm sad humanity. Not always so sad either. The people you are with become part of you, even there."

Maija was too upset to have anything more than a cup of tea. She fussed around with a length of dark yarn, but in the end unraveled it. Elizabeth bit her lip, wanting to ease the worry.

"Do you have any cards, Maija?" she asked.

"Cards? What do you want with cards?"

"My father used to make me play double solitaire with him when I was upset, or he was upset. We play very fast, that's the point. It's just something good to do sometimes."

Maija did have one deck, but didn't know how to play. Elizabeth borrowed another deck of cards from Sophie and showed Maija how the game went. Soon they were playing at breakneck speed so that there was no time to dwell on anything else. They slammed the cards on the table, cried out when they raced to put the same card on the pile, and rapidly began a new game once the old one was played out. So, for perhaps an hour, Maija had the relief of forgetting what she had seen that afternoon, and as the last card was turned, she ended genuinely exhausted.

Elizabeth now became the mother. She drew a hot bath for Maija and massaged her shoulders and back, brought her a fresh nightgown, and covered her up once she was in bed.

"Nobody has ever done this for me!" Maija said, pleased, but protesting weakly. But the heaviness of the memories stayed with her until she dropped off to sleep.

The next day came but the idea for a tapestry stayed hidden somewhere, obscured by fog, the fog outside, and the fog in Elizabeth's mind that would not lift. Unable to stay in the apartment anymore, she went for a long walk.

She walked to the top of a hill. The city was a vast sea of grayness, and she tried to recapture a tapestry she had once dreamed about, a bright center of burning reds and oranges, but it wavered and did not come. The city was a dark, brooding presence where women could be raped and stabbed, and babies could be left wailing in fear beside them.

Three young girls, arm in arm, giggled, laughing at secrets, strolling by as though it were a summer day full of sun, and Elizabeth looked at them with envy. How she wished she could laugh!

Darkness, all she could feel was darkness. Chilled, she walked home again and once more she passed Dora as she was going out.

"Hello, Dora," she said. But the girl shook her head once and moved on. And in that moment Elizabeth saw her translated into a dark sculpture, a brooding presence that was the darkness everywhere around her.

And now Elizabeth knew what she was going to do.

She dashed up the stairs three at a time, threw off her coat, and went to the wall where the yarns lay, glowing in the darkness of the day. But this time she let the brilliant colors go and instead pulled out skeins of thick natural wools, dark hemps, a skein of thick handspun Mexican brown wool still matted and peppered with flecks of grass and weed seeds. She compared them, put one back, and reached for a skein of thick wool dyed a dense orange. Then she held the wools together to see how they harmonized, and all the time she trembled inwardly for she knew she was coming closer to what she was going to create.

The thought was not entirely in her grasp. "It's not as though I were making it up but as though it were already there, and all I have to do is discover it," she thought. She must tell Maija this; it seemed important.

Different pictures, closely allied, appeared before her, but none of them was quite right. So she pulled out the drawing pad, or what was left of it, found a charcoal and began to sketch. Again she was amazed, as the charcoal seemed to know what to do.

It made a mask, a powerful dark concentration, like a mask of pain. This was right. This was where she was headed.

How to do it was the problem. She could not see it on a flat tapestry, not this. Or in three dimensions, like a sculptured head. A mask, that was it. A mask that would be complete in itself, hanging on the wall, with long dank hair descending on either side.

All she had to do now was make up a technique she had never learned. Stretching a broom handle across the tops of the looms, hers and Maija's, she began to build a black web from it. "I'm no spider," she thought, after several false starts. But finally she had made herself a frame and was on her way.

"You're working. Right? I knew it right away," Maija said when she came in. "I can tell because you're glowing. May I see it?"

Elizabeth was dying to show it to her and to tell her everything that had happened. But a voice as instinctive as the one that had directed the making of the mask told her to say nothing more and not to show the work.

"I'm sorry, Maija, but I have to do it myself."

"That's all right, Liz. That's good. Whenever you're ready."

Maija's good news was that the girl who had been attacked, though suffering with a gash across her face that would take time to heal, would live.

"And have they found out who attacked her?" Elizabeth asked.

Maija shook her head. "Who knows? Sometimes we have to be content with simply being alive."

The next two days passed in a fever, and on the third day, when Maija came home, she passed into the kitchen and then took a back step to see what she had almost missed.

The dark glowering woven mask, half-hidden behind a deliberately tangled and knotted length of hair, hung on the wall. Elizabeth had stuffed tissue paper behind it to make it more three-dimensional.

"Where did this come from?" Maija asked.

"You don't know?" Elizabeth said.

"*You* did this, Liz? *You* did it? Of course. It's Dora. Liz, it's too much. Oh let me hug you! It's so good! My dear, you are really an artist. There can't be any doubt now."

Maija had to take it off the wall and examine it. She

questioned Elizabeth about how she had done this, and how she had managed there.

"But it was really sort of accidental, Maija. If I hadn't met Dora twice in a row like that, I'd still be trying to figure out what to do."

"Come sit here at the table and I'll tell you something. Everything in life is chance. The tapestries, the paintings, music, even stories are there around us all the time in the air, at our feet, everywhere. You pass a thousand possible ideas every day between here and the street corner. It's picking them up and putting them together that counts. And so, that's what you did. And that's what makes an artist."

"Wow! I did? I am?" Elizabeth asked, joking, embarrassed and pleased, more pleased than she could tell Maija. If only I could show it to my father, she thought. But that would have to wait.

# 36

The very atmosphere celebrated Elizabeth's mask, her first genuine work, by dispelling the fog and changing to a proper July day, with warm sun and a lazy breeze. A Saturday.

"And we're going to celebrate," Maija said, "so here's a present for you."

From the back of the closet Maija reached for a package wrapped in brown paper and gave it to Elizabeth, who pulled out a long dress, a blue-purple hand-woven cotton with a trace of gold braid around the neck. The design of the dress was one Elizabeth had never seen before.

"It's Tibetan and it's been in the backroom of the Launderette as long as I can remember, so it's legally ours. If you like it, it's for you. Do you like it?"

Elizabeth put it on and felt it changing her into a sleek, feminine personage. She put on the black wig, then on an inspiration, wrapped electric blue and crimson yarns around it, making an elaborate hairpiece for herself.

"You look like a Chinese empress in a fairy tale," Maija said.

Elizabeth, too fascinated with herself to look away from the mirror, said, "It can really be done. You can be more than one person in a lifetime. Even within a year, I've been at least three!"

The "celebration" took place at a tavern that was new to Elizabeth. Maija explained there might be dancing, as folk-dance enthusiasts frequented the place. An accordionist played while the girls enjoyed soup and wine, drinking slowly in the half-darkened room. About nine o'clock, more musicians came, and the tables were pushed back against the wall while three couples got up to do a polka. Maija's lips parted; "It reminds me a little of when I was a kid," she confided to Elizabeth, "only it was not quite the same then." She laughed to cover a sadness that came and left within a second.

Then a young, somewhat beefy man, asked Maija to dance, and Elizabeth watched her whirl around the room as the polkas grew wilder and faster.

"She's very good, isn't she?" someone said to Elizabeth. "You want to dance too?"

He was blond, reminding her of Daniel Wilson, so that she hesitated, her thoughts shooting back to another Elizabeth and another time centuries away. But the young man was waiting, and she said, "Sure, why not?"

She had never done this before and warned the young man, Joe, that she might be awkward. "There's nothing to it," he said, "your feet will know just what to do!"

And it was true. He whirled her around, tossed her in the air, danced around her while she looked to see what the others were doing. They ended breathless and flushed with excitement. Elizabeth laughed at the incongruity of it all, the proper Elizabeth van Vliet dressed as a kooky Chinese empress dancing Polish polkas with a young man who told her he was a pile driver. And all this to celebrate a tapestry she had just made!

She could not dance enough, and Joe was satisfied to stay with her all evening. As they were getting ready to leave, he asked if he could see her the next day, maybe take her riding down the coast. She looked at Maija questioningly, and Joe said he had a good friend; all four of them could go. But Maija shook her head.

"I'm sorry," she said regretfully but with a certain finality, "but we have other plans for tomorrow."

Elizabeth held out her hand to Joe. "I enjoyed it so much. And I'm sorry about tomorrow. Maybe we'll be back sometime."

The music stayed with her long after they got home. As she wiped off the eye make-up she had used and hung up the new dress, she thought how nothing in the world could take the place of being with a man. And she wondered what was so important the next day, that Maija had so definitely turned down the invitation.

"It will be something good anyway. Maija doesn't lie," she told herself, and then the lilting music echoed again in her ears, and she fell asleep dreaming of whirling around and around and around down a long, endless corridor.

# 37

Waking to the most delicious summer morning she had yet experienced in San Francisco, Elizabeth wished Maija had not been so abrupt with Joe the night before and that presently, in an hour or so, Joe and a friend would honk the horn below and the four of them would drive down the coast along the blue-green waters of the ocean. What sort of special plan did Maija have, she wondered.

"Let's dress up," Maija said. Dressing up in the day-time was a joke, Elizabeth thought, a cotton shirt over pants for Maija and the Tibetan dress for her, which now had a taint of being a leftover from the Launderette. Maija, putting the picnic lunch together, was humming away. "I'm spoiled. I'm still a nasty little girl," Elizabeth thought and made up her mind to enjoy the day, no matter what.

But when they had bussed to Land's End and walked through the formal open area around the museum, Elizabeth noticed all the lovers everywhere, the sweet thirteen-year-old kids hand in hand, the older married-looking couple who seemed happy enough, and even one bent-over old couple sitting in the sun. Maija chattered without noticing. "Come, Liz, I really do have a surprise for you, you know."

Inside the museum three large rooms were given over to a new exhibition of fiber sculpture, large woven works that either stood by themselves or hung on the walls, most of the pieces so enormous that they needed a museum to do them justice.

Immediately, at first sight of this collection, everything else fell out of Elizabeth's mind and she could only stop in admiration.

"These are very well-known works for the most part, what you might call the modern classics of contemporary weaving. Most of these have already been displayed in world famous exhibitions, at Lausanne and elsewhere."

"I've seen that one in photographs and that one too," Elizabeth said as she recognized them, "but they are so much bigger and stronger when you actually see them as they are."

Slowly the girls walked between woven columns that hung from the ceiling. A darkly stained blue construction of rope, yarn and other fibers was suspended in the middle of the room, like a fantastic flying ship or a fabulous bird trailing long blue threads. In another room huge coils of rope wrapped and twisted themselves in tortured writhings like an octopus in pain. A free-standing sculpture made of woven hemp, joined, seamed and slashed, which suggested deeper and deeper folds, reminded Elizabeth of an orange jungle plant gone wild.

Speechless, she turned to Maija. "What is it, weaving or sculpture? It's so different from what we do."

"It's a kind of weaving, coming of age. It's also sculpture. Some of these pieces are very profound, I think. And important."

They walked around the exhibition, the first time to look and the second time for Maija to point out how this one was managed or how that one was manipulated to create a certain effect, to dismiss several of them as sick, incompetent mediocrities and to praise others. In the last room Maija paused before what seemed to be a particularly complicated arc winging through space.

"I worked on that one," she said simply.

"You did? But your work doesn't look like that at all."

"Ha! Just because you see me working flat doesn't mean I can't be three-dimensional. We had some dandy problems with that one, Monica and I. It was mostly hers, but you see, we were together on a small island near Wales . . ."

Maija's voice drifted off, and then Elizabeth knew she was alone and would not, could not be followed. Instantly she was jealous of the Monica who could do such amazing feats of sculpture, spending a summer with Maija.

"Maija, I want to learn to work like this, without the loom. Please, will you let me?"

"How impatient you are! Your mask was a beginning."

"That mask! Now it seems tiny and puny. So juvenile."

Maija put her finger to Elizabeth's lips. "No, not at all. It's a beautiful piece of work. Size isn't everything, nor is being complicated and full of engineering tricks. Anyway, you mustn't compare your work with anyone else's. You do what is right for you. That's enough."

They looked at the show once more and then strolled

out, found a daisy-spotted meadow not too far away, and opened their lunch. Gulls flew past. Images of great works began to pass through Elizabeth's mind. Oh, the things she was going to do!

Later that day, Maija took some long pieces of wood from the porch in back of the apartment, found a hammer and nails, and told Elizabeth to construct a loom by the window.

"You want me to do that? But how?" Elizabeth said.

"That's your worry," Maija said.

"But I want to do non-loom things, like we saw today."

"You will. When the time comes. First you need a good foundation. These flat wall tapestries you are learning to do are classic, as classic as the music of Bach or Mozart. Naturally, we shall design them as people living today, not as if we lived in another century. But once you learn to control a flat area such as this and design for it, you are well on your way. Liz, you'll need a metal support over in that corner or it won't hold."

"But Maija, I have an idea for a free-standing, or rather a suspended figure. It's sort of a big mama-type woman and we can use wires to make it rounded. I think it could really be good."

"It could. When you get an idea like that, make a sketch of it and put it away, don't throw it away. Let it develop in your subconscious. If it's any good, it won't rot, believe me. But right now, I have a set of problems for you to solve. In a way it's a test for you. In other words, I'll give you a number of requirements, including all the techniques we've learned, and it's going to be up to you to arrange them in a pattern that works in color and design."

"But Maija, I've been doing that," Elizabeth pouted.

"I'm the teacher and you're the student. Take it or leave it," Maija said, firmly and calmly, testing the strength of Elizabeth's loom. Then she sat down on the floor and proceeded to write in a straight even list what Elizabeth was required to include in her new work. "It's really very simple, and in a sense you haven't done this before. When you finish, I'll give you a diploma with a gold seal!"

"Just what I need!" Elizabeth said. She sighed and continued to work on the new loom.

# 38

Again Elizabeth struggled with a design, tearing off the pages of the newsprint pad with soft mutterings and sounds of disgust, wanting Maija to hear and yet knowing that giving way to rage would only poison the room where Maija, humming, wove on *The Phoenix* with spider dexterity. That afternoon Elizabeth walked for two hours and wasted a third in a music store where she listened to the records she used to like. Now she found them dull.

Was she restless? Bored? Was it the summer mildness in the air that made the hours when Maija was gone interminable? At least Maija had someone or something. Twice since her first night away from the apartment she had called to say she wouldn't be home until midnight or so. But she never talked about where she went, and Elizabeth, looking at her and on the verge of asking, never quite dared to find out. Now in the long afternoons Elizabeth felt herself longing for something, she did not know what.

But the mornings with Maija were always fresh and alert. Maija seemed to know just when to come off her stool and stand close to Elizabeth to see what she had been drawing, to suggest where the pattern could be intensified, or to show her how she could use mirrors to help in designing.

"You mustn't be so grim. Some of it is a kind of game, like a fugue. Do you know any Bach fugues? Well, what he used to do was this . . ."

And Maija would describe the devices he used while Elizabeth looked on in amazement that this girl, who couldn't even sing the simplest polka on key, knew how music was put together. Maija sang a theme from a fugue, and Elizabeth burst out laughing; it sounded like a polka. Maija laughed too.

At last the design was completed, drawn on butcher paper the exact size it would be when complete. Now Elizabeth had to choose her colors. All along she had suspected that after the starkness of the mask, she would plunge into blazing reds, oranges and purples. Yet her hands, knowing better, chose pale colors, off-whites, quiet golds, a strand of fog blue and a brief touch of orange.

"You have a feeling for colors, something that comes naturally, no matter how much you learn about color in books," Maija said. She did not compliment Elizabeth very often and still criticized her work harshly but honestly, and so Elizabeth was pleased.

"They are my father's colors," she said quietly, and

a longing to see him again came on her so intensely that she went into the bathroom so that Maija would not see the tears.

The mornings were the best time, watching the light change from early fog to a gradual glow of summer light. Sometimes the summer never came — San Francisco being a coastal city and not a slave to the seasons — and then the fog caressed the houses, softening the city with a gray hush.

Elizabeth was too proud to complain of the malaise she suffered in the long hours of the afternoon and evening, but Maija knew. As Elizabeth, now interested in working out the problems, tried to make her fingers fly as easily as Maija's, Maija sometimes broke the silence with stories, or something she remembered from her childhood, or an anecdote about what seemed to Elizabeth the most travel-packed experience anyone could have.

"When I was studying in Norway, I had to do a very realistic finely worked sample of tapestry, a fifteenth-century sort of thing, a flower with a drop of dew on the leaves. That drop of dew took twelve different shades of white and gray. I almost went out of my mind, matching the colors. It took me a week to do a piece ten by twelve inches."

"Will I have to do that?"

"No, Liz, don't worry. I want you to appreciate what you are doing, that's all."

Elizabeth counted her blessings: Maija's good nature, her own increasing skill, the pleasant lunches they took in the warm noon sun on the small landing at the head of the outside stairs. When it was time for

Maija to go each day, Elizabeth dreaded the lonely afternoons, yet she was too proud to complain.

A long lonely afternoon, a long evening until Maija's return. Sophie, kind good Sophie, understood the heaviness of Elizabeth's solitude and sometimes knocked on the door to bring her little cakes or an eggplant concoction from her native Yugoslavia which she swore was like caviar. Now and then she said Elizabeth must come over and see this darling new dog who had come to be groomed. And then there would be still another old lady to meet, or even an old man, and the usual cup of tea in a glass.

However much Sophie was careful not to intrude, there came an afternoon when she found Elizabeth sitting by the window and gazing out. Then she blurted out her concern. "Listen to me now, Elizabeth. Your father wants you home. Every day is in the paper he wants you home. And your mother. So what foolishness to stay here. Maija is a nice girl, yes, but she is not your mother and you are such a young girl, almost a baby."

"I know, Sophie. I'd like to let them know I'm all right. But I can't go back, not yet. Someday it will be time and I'll do it."

But Sophie sighed on. "Someday could be too late. Your poor mother, I know how she feels. If only I had a daughter like you . . ."

Loneliness must be obvious, Elizabeth thought, as though someone painted it on you like a color. And she was touched that the few people she knew seemed to understand it and to care.

Hardly a day passed that Nicholas didn't invite Elizabeth to play checkers with him or take him for a walk. More than once Boris took her along with

Nicholas to the zoo or, the aquarium as an afternoon treat.

Even Mr. Hommada took her hand one day and looked in her face. "What you need, Elizabeth, is someone to love, something small and soft. I have just the thing. Come and see. You like kittens, Elizabeth?"

In the back of the store a gray striped cat lay nursing five kittens. Elizabeth picked one up, stroked its soft fur, and held it close.

"It just cuddles to me," she said. "Oh, could you spare it, Mr. Hommada?"

"Sparing it is not my problem," he said. "Let's let her stay with her mama for another week, and then you may come and have her. She's yours!"

"I'll call her Lotus," Elizabeth said.

"Good Lord," Maija said when Elizabeth told her that evening, "have you ever seen a cat play with yarn? It's suicide."

But when she saw Elizabeth's face fall, she relented. "All right, she'll be good company. But you will be her mother and you'll be responsible — for everything. You understand?"

"Oh, Maija. You *are* wonderful. I love you. I really do."

"I love you too but I'm starving. Which reminds me, tomorrow night we're invited to dinner at Katina's."

Elizabeth was aware that Maija created excuses to keep her from taking on more solitude than she was able to manage, but she had never heard of Katina. "Who's she?"

"I've never mentioned her to you? She's an unbelievable young woman, a weaver who's gone into natural dyes and spinning and carding as well. In fact, she's getting to be an expert. She'll have to be part of The

Studio when it gets going. In the meantime, I need some more wool dyed, so you'll have a chance to look her over."

Elizabeth could never quite believe in The Studio, that harebrained utopia of Maija's, but she went along with the dream and looked forward to the next night.

"Don't swing your bag like that," Maija warned. "This is Mugland, even worse than the rest of the city. Jungle all the way."

They had taken the bus down Page Street, had transferred to the Mission District, and finally walked under the freeway to get to the building where Katina lived. "It's like a stage set for a murder," Elizabeth said as she clung to Maija; she was relieved when at last they stepped inside the doorway of what might once have been a warehouse. The figure of a girl appeared at the top of the stairs, the light throwing an enormous black shadow on the wall.

"Come on up. I've been waiting for you!"

Maija introduced Elizabeth proudly, as though she were showing her off, while Elizabeth tried not to stare at Katina who was young and even pretty, but huge, a long gathered skirt making her look even more massive. Her hair was wound around her head in a thick braid, and as they walked into the studio, a black cat jumped to Katina's shoulder and sat there, blinking at Elizabeth with golden eyes. She's a witch, Elizabeth thought to herself.

It really must have been a warehouse, thought Elizabeth, looking at the unusually high ceilings and rough wooden walls. Long hanks of dyed yarns swung gently from the ceiling, the colors emerging out of the darkness above and lit delicately and unevenly by the light of two table lamps made from old lanterns. Whites and off-whites looped in thick fleecy ropes; from another rafter red and orange lengths of thick wool glowed, and in the far corner a glimmer of blues and greens caught the light from time to time. While Maija and Katina settled themselves on immense floor cushions and sipped wine as they talked, Elizabeth sat quietly by like a good child gone out visiting with her mother. Again and again her eyes were drawn to the corners of the studio where more yarns swung gently; she could almost feel the touch of them in her fingers.

"I hear you're into tapestry. How are you getting on?" Katina asked.

"All right, I guess," Elizabeth said blushing, a schoolgirl questioned by adults. How is school? What are you studying? Maija sensed her embarrassment.

"My best student. My only student, too, of course. Do you suppose, Katina, that you could show her what you're doing?"

"I'd love to, but let's have dinner first. I think we'll have it here."

Katina shifted with ease as she moved her heavy bulk to get up. If someone had told Elizabeth that Katina could dance lightly on her toes with the grace that some large women have, she would not have been surprised. Katina's vast skirt was pinned together with safety pins and Elizabeth noticed her large bare feet, not particularly clean. Elizabeth began to see her in her mind's eye as a tapestry, a voluminous three-dimensional portrait with a cat on her shoulder and another following at her heels.

The pottery of savory stew that she brought in smelled of wine and herbs, a brew made by a skillful witch. Maija cared little for cooking, but Elizabeth had sometimes enjoyed it, and now she felt humble, sure that Katina was a master cook, a supreme artist with flavors and textures. The three girls sat on the floor at the low table, followed Katina's example of dunking French bread in the stew, and finished the meal with a bowl of fruit.

I am beginning to love this place, Elizabeth thought, thinking of the straw baskets and wooden tubs that were neatly placed along the further wall, the shelves of yarns, the small Franklin stove glowing and in the kitchen, something, not food, simmering in a huge pot on one of the burners. She felt she was being watched, and looking up, she saw one cat crouched on a beam looking down at her, and in the far corner, almost hidden in the shadows, another one blinking and watching. Would she ever be able to live in an ordinary house again?

"If you want the grand tour, let's go," Katina said. They walked to the far end of the room and Katina lifted some raw wool from a large basket and handed it to Elizabeth, lumps of dirt, weeds and all, to say nothing of its distinct greasy feel.

"That's the lanolin," Katina explained and then went on to describe how it had to be washed, carded, and spun. Picking up her carding boards, she showed how easily the wool fibers could be fluffed and swept into one straight direction. Reaching for a spindle, she then wove the fluffy length of fibers into yarn, sometimes spinning it out to the thickness of a thread, at other times controlling it to produce a fiber half an inch thick and perfectly smooth. And Elizabeth was even more fascinated when Katina deftly spun a fiber that alternated from thin to thick dimensions with perfect control. Elizabeth had never understood these processes when she studied them in grammar school, and she was amazed not only that they required so much skill but that there was such a ritual in it.

"I'd love to know how to do that," she said.

"Nothing to it," Katina said, "if you don't mind practicing a few hours every day — for a few years!"

The other baskets were filled with dried flowers, grasses, roots and weeds. A tawny cat meowed and jumped as Katina bent down to pick up a few weeds. "I'll be boiling these to make dyes. Believe it, but I don't think you will, this dull green plant produces the most delicate pink you ever want to see. And this basket has hundreds of marigold heads that will make a good orange-yellow, or maybe a soft yellow or an amber brown. It depends on the *mordant* or chemicals you use with it. Throw in a rusty nail and you get a different color! See?"

She moved to the kitchen, actually a niche in part of the big room where two pots bubbled on the stove. Katina lifted masses of dyeing wool with a large wooden spoon. Again Elizabeth had the feeling that even if Katina were not a witch, she possessed supernatural skills. All the while Katina talked, giving Maija and Elizabeth handfuls of different wool to feel and explaining how she had run across some long-haired goats in Siskiyou County "with fibers that long!" She had found the owners and contracted to get some of that goat hair. Then she asked if they would like tea now, for she was all talked out.

"Impossible!" Maija joked, putting her arm around Katina.

As the three of them sat on the cushions around the low table once more, Elizabeth felt a kinship between

194

Maija and Katina, something that came from their being so much a part of their work. And she wondered if someday she too would feel this kind of passion.

"Shall I read the tea leaves?" Katina asked.

"Oh, please!" Elizabeth cried, giving her her cup. Katina studied the bottom of the cup in the lamplight. "I see some triumphs, something triumphal, I don't know what. And a shadow, but I can't make it out. Travel, Liz, a big trip within the next six months. That's about it for now."

"Do mine, will you Katina? You're so fabulous. You always get things right."

Katina took Maija's cup over to the light, but her smile faded as she peered into the cup. She didn't say anything.

"Well?"

"The light's bad in here. I can't make it out. Anyway, these cups . . . Steve made them . . . have such a dark glaze I can't even see the tea leaves. Next time, okay?"

They began to discuss matters that Elizabeth described to herself as gossip, talking about people she didn't know. And then it was time to go, to rush, in fact, in order to catch the bus. From the bottom of the stairs the girls looked up to wave goodbye and to say thank you, while Katina, firmly planted on the top step, urged them to come again.

"Do you suppose she's lonely?" Elizabeth asked on the way home.

"I never thought about it. No, I think she's learned to live with herself."

"Anyway," Elizabeth said, "by all means, she has to be part of The Studio."

She talked as though she actually believed in it!

## 39

Elizabeth believed everything Maija said. And Maija said the one thing she could always count on was change, and that even the afternoon and evening loneliness she suffered from now would not be a problem forever. It would solve itself and most likely there would be new problems. "Like hiking through a mountainous country, you climb one hill only to see another in front of you."

And the intensity of the loneliness did pass, although there was still a feeling of emptiness Elizabeth could not understand.

But she was learning to handle loneliness. Taking Nicholas for a walk to the Japanese Center to look at the fish was a way of cheating the loneliness, and more than once she had sat in the dusk with Sophie, listening to stories about her girlhood in Yugoslavia. Sometimes, while informally teaching Elizabeth how to comb a dog's hair and trim his nails, Sophie talked about her departed husband. Was he dead or had he left her? Was he the "low-down skunk" Sophie cursed one day or the prince she sighed about the next? More than once Sophie had held her poodle close to her and whispered in the soft ear, "We like dogs better than people, don't we, Putzi?"

It was also Sophie who kept urging her to call her father, call her mother, make up with them, go home, find a good husband, have babies.

"You can even use my phone. I'll treat you to the call, three minutes. Your poor mother! Whatever you've done, she'll forgive you."

"But I haven't done anything really bad."

Sophie tsk-tsked and shook her head like a mother. And the kitten, that dear kitten. "How would I ever get along without you?" Elizabeth whispered to it, holding the soft little creature against her cheek. Lotus attacked her tapestry, became entangled in a skein of wool that took half an hour to straighten out, and purred for Elizabeth, who scolded her but spoiled her with tidbits.

One afternoon as she wrestled with the difficult design problem Maija had given her, a knock on the door interrupted her train of thought. "Just a minute," she called with a touch of impatience. But when she put down her bobbin with a sigh and opened the door, she found herself facing Maija's man. It must be the same. She was aware immediately of the dark eyes, the air of intelligence and his arms full of spring flowers that had obviously come from a florist. Iris, calendula, marguerites, lilies of the valley, hyacinth . . . they were luminous enough to light the dark hall.

"You must be Elizabeth?" Such a gentle voice, the kind her mother would praise as being cultivated.

"Yes," she said, her eyes traveling from the olive, perhaps Semitic face, to the burst of flower color and back.

"I'm David Kazarian. I'd like to leave these for Maija. Would you mind putting them in water? There's a note in there for her."

"She'll be very pleased. Do you want to come in?"

"I'd love to take a peek at *The Phoenix*, if I may. It

197

really is coming along, isn't it? A gorgeous thing. Do you like it, Elizabeth?"

"It's fantastic," she said shyly as if one couldn't praise it enough.

"I hear you're doing some splendid things too."

"Oh it's just . . ." she blushed and shrugged her shoulders as if what she did was nothing. It was his presence, the kind steady eyes, the casual but carefully ordered clothes he wore, and the gentle voice that made her blush. So this was Maija's man! Incredible, she thought. He thanked Elizabeth for taking care of the flowers and left. She ran to the window and looked below as he crossed the street, thin and slightly stooped, ever so slightly, and eased his way into the car she had seen the last time he called for Maija.

Obediently she put the lovely blooms in a hand-thrown pot, held the small envelope up to the light, wondered if she should steam it open and read what was inside, then with sudden shame put it beside the flowers.

The room seemed emptier than ever. Lotus, who had been sleeping in a warm place near the stove, leaped to her shoulder and purred. "You're nice, kitty, but I need something more. Someone."

She sat at the loom and tried to go on with her work, but the silence fell around her, heavy and stifling. If only she had some music, if only she could hear the sound of people's voices. . . .

But that wasn't so difficult. A radio, that would do it. If only she hadn't forgotten to take the one her father had given her. Maija had spoken several times about "a sea of silence where you could feel yourself breathing and learn that you were there." Well, Maija had people to talk with all afternoon and evening, and Maija got flowers from men like David Kazarian.

All right, she could make a few decisions too. Letting her bobbin fall to the floor, she went to the bedroom, pulled the suitcase from under her bed, and came upon the wallet she had put away with her savings. One hundred and eighty-two dollars and change. How much did a radio cost? Well, what was money for anyway? Whatever it cost, it would cost.

She put on the black wig, looked at herself, sullen and unsmiling, in the mirror, and walked down the stairs and into the street. She hesitated before the hardware store at the corner and then passed it; it was too close to home. As she walked on, she justified herself in her thoughts.

Maybe Maija wasn't that much different from Lorene in some ways. She was a teacher. Everything had to be correct and that was all that mattered. Maija should be in a convent, she told herself, and then remembered the glowing flowers. Was she jealous?

Maybe so.

But not of Maija. No, she loved Maija. It was just that it was impossible to worship someone all the time. And anyway, she, Elizabeth, wasn't a puritan, and if she wanted the company of a radio, surely that was her right.

At the next music store she asked the clerk to show her radios. She used such a defiant tone that he looked at her in astonishment. Ten minutes later she walked out, fifteen dollars poorer, with a small transistor tucked in her bag.

On the way home she continued to think about her

situation. Maija demanded too much of her. It was Elizabeth's right to have music. Well, wasn't it?

Yet, when she passed a Viennese bakery, the display of tarts and confections as perfect as frothy sculptures made her wish Maija were there. Maija's weakness was to love sweets and her strength was to say no, because she was afraid of getting fat. She is really thin, not an ounce of fat on her, and a cream puff or tart would please her, it really would, Elizabeth thought. And so she went into the store and finally decided on a small pie, a mosaic of fruits, mostly apricots and strawberries, covered with a glaze and a rim of whipped cream around the edge. Two and a half dollars was high, but it made the gift all the more rare. She carried the flat white pastry box home with a feeling of pleasure.

Yet even her present didn't settle the restless impatience she felt, this nameless desire she couldn't define. She found herself resenting Maija, Maija who was always so full of good spirits and courage, Maija who never complained or suffered. Did Maija expect her, Elizabeth, to be such a saint?

"I wish the day were over," she thought. With neither the summer sun warming her nor the comforting privacy of the fog wrapping around her, the wind blew dismally. The skies admitted nothing, and the streets were becoming unusually ugly with dirty papers and trash blowing around. It was a part of town she had not walked through before, and now she realized that her long walk, essentially a large circle, had led her close to the Launderette where Maija worked. What if she should drop in?

An ugliness of suspicion came over her. Maybe Maija was so insistent about her not visiting because she wasn't there at all. Perhaps she was out somewhere

200

with David Kazarian, or with someone else. Fictions filled her mind.

She was so close to the place that it wouldn't really matter if she took a quick peek. As Maija had described it, the building stood in a vacant block filled with trash and rocks, a last tooth in a gaping mouth.

She stood cautiously outside the building under the chipped sign that said *Super-Launderette*. Signs and posters tattered by the wind and marred by ugly graffiti covered the outside walls. But inside the place was steamy and white, an ordered place. Maija herself had whitewashed the walls and covered them with a row of travel posters of Mexico and Africa, suggesting a brighter world somewhere else. Mothers slumped in chairs reading newspapers or looking ahead blankly, while several small children darted around playing hide and seek. At last Elizabeth found Maija, kneeling in back of an outworn washing machine, a screwdriver in her hand and a box of tools open at her feet. Then, as a black woman, an old grandmother, began to take sheets from a dryer, Maija put down her tools and went over to help her fold them. The two stood apart, shaking and folding the sheets and talking easily, like neighbors in a sunny backyard talking. Maija lifted the woman's laundry basket, put it on the wagon, and helped her through the door with it while Elizabeth flattened against the wall.

When she looked inside again, Maija was holding a crying baby and bouncing him gently while his mother took the damp clothes from a washer to the dryer. Then, when the mother took her baby again, Maija went back to her tools and the washing machine. She wore a white cotton kerchief on her head, the points falling loose like a nun's headcovering. Maija carried around a tray of soaps and bleaches in paper cups, and Elizabeth thought she looked like a priestess carrying the sacrament.

Chastened because of her previous suspicions, Elizabeth turned to go home. She would do all the housecleaning now and not resent it anymore. She would make a good soup for Maija's dinner. She would finish the dull tapestry in less than a week to surprise her. Maija was good, so very good. Hadn't she taken in Elizabeth when there wasn't another soul she could go to?

She was thinking all this so earnestly that she did not realize two young men were following her, their eyes never leaving her for a second.

"Hey, sistah, what's the hurry? You wanna get home? Wheah you goin'?"

"Maybe you' lost, huh? We he'p you find the way."

She turned around and froze with fear. Her mouth opened but the scream was soundless as she stared at the two leering young men. They laughed and she could sense the hatred behind the sound. She stood rooted to the sidewalk as in a nightmare. The street was empty except for two small children far away, and the vacant lot seemed to stretch out forever. The men took a step toward her and immediately she turned and ran. They joked between themselves as they followed; they were long-legged and ran easily, yet she seemed to be running in one place, as in a dream. Her heart thumped unnaturally. She knew herself as a small harmless animal, a young deer or a rabbit being chased.

In desperation she dashed across the street, barely missing a massive truck. The driver yelled at her to look where she was goin', but his truck stopped her pursuers long enough so that she could reach Geary Street; she said thank God for the green light that let her dash across the wide street to safety, and she did not look back to see but knew that her pursuers had given up.

Once home, she collapsed on a chair and shook for several minutes, then caught her breath, and went to dash cold water on her face. The little apartment had never seemed more like a haven. "God bless our happy home," she quoted almost hysterically, recalling a cheap print of a sampler containing those words that had been in Lorene's kitchen. But it was blessed, she knew. She would not abandon it again.

Flooded with good intentions she swept the floors, cleaned the refrigerator, and cut vegetables for the curry that Maija liked so well. It was then that she remembered the radio she had bought. A little music was all she needed to keep her company. The first station she found played a frenetic rock and roll; she had forgotten how coarse a disc jockey could be. The station close by was a talk program, a woman was yelling across the airwaves something about high prices, the hysteria coming through more clearly than the words; another station played the songs she had liked only last year, but they now seemed insipid. At last she found a good music station, but after a few minutes of Brahms, it faded away.

"So much for that!" she said out loud, turning it off decisively. Then she put the radio and the money she hadn't spent back in the bottom of the suitcase under her bed. Silence said more, after all.

When Maija came in, she found a scrubbed Elizabeth in a scrubbed kitchen, fussing with biscuits.

"Maija, these flowers came for you!" She gave her the vase.

"For me?" Joyful, Maija buried her face in the

fragrant blooms and looked at Elizabeth with joy beaming.

"And this card goes with it," Elizabeth said, handing her the envelope.

Maija opened it, still joyful, and almost immediately the happiness fled and tears filled her eyes. She turned to brush them away, but Elizabeth had seen them. Maija stood with her face in her hands and her shoulders quivered. When she turned around again, she spoke with a forced calm. "I'm sorry. It's nothing really. Let's have dinner. You've been working hard!"

All through dinner, Elizabeth waited for Maija to talk about the note, but she would not ask, and Maija, making small talk, would not tell. The girls sat opposite one another, but the flowers were there between them, keeping them apart. Sensing this, Maija said, "I can't see you with these in the way," and moved the vase of flowers into the other room. Again, Elizabeth felt at peace.

# 40

"Maija, sometimes I think you're as contradictory as I am, and it's such a relief. I'm not alone."

Maija told her to have a nice visit with Katina. And then she was on her way.

As the bus drove by Union Square, Elizabeth realized it was a long time since she had been there, so when it stopped, she got off and strolled through the familiar little park. The afternoon was full of benevolent sunlight, the pigeons flew overhead, and the park seemed different now than when she had been a little girl and her mother had taken her to the city to shop. I. Magnin's, the large store which she once believed was a marble palace, still stood across the street. Three girls, probably not much older than she, clicked by, their shoes stylishly heeled and their short dresses ending exactly where their long legs would show to the greatest advantage. Recently washed hair glistened in the sunlight, and Elizabeth, catching snatches of their conversation, wished suddenly she were one of them. Her wig had never seemed more dull and artificial, but Maija had warned it was too early to shed it, and now her jeans and jersey mortified her with their shabbiness.

Elizabeth crossed the street and walked by the windows slowly. In one window two well-groomed mannequins looked up at a backdrop of a European castle; in the next window a mother sunned herself on a beach while her two children built a sand castle; and in the window around the corner, figures in mauve and champagne chiffons seemed to float through a garden party. Elizabeth stood there caught between two worlds, seeing herself quite easily in an afternoon frock sprigged with flowers and a wide straw hat, yet the reflection of herself in worn jeans and an unbecoming wig was more truthful.

Yet she did not hesitate to walk into the store. She stood on the familiar marble floors and was somehow surprised to see herself in mirrors all around. She breathed in the fragrance of perfumes and soaps, lingered over the pretty labels with their French names, and remembered how, when she was a little girl, the saleswoman sprayed her with colognes and touched perfume behind her ears, remarking on what a lovely child she was and where did she get such a translucent skin and large gray eyes!

She wandered to the accessory department, where silk scarves and hand bags of fine leather were casually displayed, so soft to the touch that she caught her breath. She was like her mother after all, in love with beautiful things, the luxuries that cost too much.

"May I help you?" the saleslady in a well-cut gray frock with an impeccable white collar asked, her tone implying, "What is somebody like you doing here?" Elizabeth moved toward the door, angry and apologetic, yet before going out, an impulse made her turn around.

A woman, her back toward Elizabeth, had moved to the same hand bag counter and stood there while her white hands fluttered through a pile of scarves. The green silk suit was familiar, and the slope of the shoulders. "My mother," Elizabeth murmured wonderingly, as though she came from a distant planet.

Immediately she felt she must run over and say hello, but she stood rooted to the spot. Her mother was putting on weight, she noticed, and when she turned, her profile seemed to droop. The salesgirl who had been so cold to Elizabeth spoke to her mother and her lips lifted in an automatic smile; for a moment the ghost of past charm returned, then left. Her mother was getting old, a terrible thing to realize, because she had always seemed so timeless. The urge to run over returned; Elizabeth saw herself putting her arms around her mother and saying, "Mummy, it's not too late. Come live with me now and we'll get Daddy back, and then we can all be together again."

206

Humpty-dumpty. Too late.

Her mother, feeling that someone was looking at her, turned around and her gaze passed over Elizabeth and returned to the scarves. What was that phrase, Elizabeth wondered, "Your own mother wouldn't know you!" No, her mother didn't know her. Had she changed so much in so short a time? Could something as silly as an obvious wig fool her mother?

Troubled, she made her way to Katina's.

# 41

All week long, she was haunted by the image of her mother, and twice she had been on the verge of telephoning. But it wasn't time, not yet.

As she worked on her loom during the long mornings, she wondered if perhaps her mother made a habit of coming to the city to shop on Wednesdays. For all her flightiness, her mother followed certain patterns of order. So the following Wednesday afternoon Elizabeth dressed in the new clothes her mother had bought her in May and brushed her newly washed hair until it shone. One of these days she would give the wig to Nicholas to play with, for she had decided firmly she wasn't going to wear it anymore; if she were discovered, that was that, although she doubted it would happen. In any event, as she looked in the mirror she was neither Elizabeth Bird nor the other Elizabeth but someone in between. And this time, if her mother were there, she would recognize her. As she swung onto the bus, she became more and more assured that soon she'd be seeing her mother.

But Elizabeth's mother was nowhere to be seen on the first floor, or the second or the third, nowhere wandering around half-heartedly or aimlessly looking through the lingerie. Tears of disappointment welled in Elizabeth's eyes as the elevator settled on the ground floor. Well, it had been a foolish thing to do.

Outside, over the hum of the traffic and the sound of people talking as they wandered along the sidewalks, Elizabeth thought she heard a violin. She was wedged up against the garden-party window, and there she stood, content to listen to the music. It seemed to echo her sadness.

Looking over the crowd, she found the violinist, a tall young man who scowled furiously as he labored over a difficult passage. Long blond hair fell over his face, and he frequently had to shake his head to get it out of his eyes. Occasionally people stopped to throw odd bits of change into his open violin case. Sometimes he said thanks, then, scowling again, would return right away to his music; and when a melodious passage began . . . imagine playing Beethoven in front of I. Magnin's! . . . he relaxed and swayed with the music. One time he looked up to give her an intense glance, but catching her eye, looked down at his music. Later he looked up again, and when he found she was still there watching him, he nodded as if to acknowledge her presence. When the concerto ended, he looked down modestly while she led the applause.

Now he's really showing off, she thought, as he embarked on an involved Bach sonata. But when some of the chords did not quite ring true, he stopped to figure them out, a note at a time, then went off into a series of thirds that sounded like exercises. He acted as if he were alone in a practice room, but it didn't matter to the public; ladies with shopping boxes walked, some without noticing him, others tossing change in his case. He went back to the sonata, and as he finished the first movement, a bearded man, not quite as young, joined him with a cello. He set up a music stand and a small stool, and the two musicians talked amiably while he tuned his cello. Then the violinist scooped the money from his violin case, put away the violin, left it with the cellist, and worked his way over to Elizabeth. Already the bouncing sounds of the cello were giving life to the sidewalk.

"Hi! Come on, let's get some coffee."

He took her hand and pulled her through the crowd, striding ahead on long legs. He knew a small restaurant tucked away in the next block, and soon they sat opposite each other at a small table.

His name was Eric Anderson and hers Elizabeth Bird.

Where did he come from? Lincoln, Nebraska.

Elizabeth laughed.

"What's the big joke?"

"Nothing, really. It's nothing. I once knew someone from there."

Her mother was already forgotten. Her spirits were dancing; it was a summer day, she was young, her hair was long, pale blond and beautiful, and there she was sitting with an exciting young man in a San Francisco restaurant. He asked a question, then she asked him a question, and all the while they were looking at each other, testing each other, judging.

She was satisfied that he was a serious person, a

former law student turned musician who would very soon be trying for a place in a symphony. The street, he said, was a godsend. "Imagine being so well paid for practicing!"

And Elizabeth felt a pride, though she spoke shyly, when she explained that she was studying weaving and tapestry. She said little, genuinely admiring him for doing so well with his violin. "If only I could play, my father would be so happy. I'd be happy too. But then . . ."

"You're perfect just as you are, Liz. But I have to get back. Look, can you be there tomorrow? I want to see you again."

She promised to be there the next day. He strode off, a serious young man, and when he was out of sight she rushed home. There was so much work to be done before Maija showed up.

# 42

"You're looking a little happier these days," Maija said. That's because your work is coming along so well. You even look different."

Elizabeth, blushing, laughed it off. She could not very well tell Maija — yet there was no reason not to tell her — that ten minutes after Maija left to help old ladies sort their laundry, she would be on her way to Eric's as she had been almost every day for a week. "I'll tell her soon," Elizabeth promised herself so as not to feel guilty, but not today.

Eric met her at the door, kissed her, and put a glass of wine in her hand. The deep, sonorous singing of Phillip's cello in the sun-drenched sitting room where he taught his pupils made talking difficult. It didn't matter. Elizabeth sank into one of the unmatching leather easy chairs, and Eric perched on a stool, never taking his eyes from her.

"I do love it here. It's the kind of place I'd like to live in. I love that modern painting, and that great quilt you have on the ceiling, and all your books and music and old pipes and that stuffed owl. It's all mixed up, and yet it makes sense. It's warm. Where we live, it's like . . ."

"A convent!" Eric finished for her.

"I wouldn't say that. Not exactly. In fact sometimes Maija can get awfully silly. And she sings in the bath, out of tune and loud. But mostly . . ." she was being unfair and unfaithful. "No, Eric, I love it there, I really do. And Maija is an angel. It's just that this is all . . . well, so easy and comfortable. And I wish Phillip weren't married so he could meet Maija. . . ."

"What a dreamer you are! In two weeks his Jeannie will be back. And I will be out, probably in Los Angeles."

"You didn't tell me that. When, Eric? It's marvelous but I'll miss you."

"It's not a sure thing yet. But there's no reason why you can't come with me."

"I couldn't do that, you know."

He leaned forward easily and spoke clearly, in order to be heard above the sound of Phillip, who was sawing away on his cello and singing along with it.

"Damn him. He doesn't need to practice all the time.

Liz, why won't he leave us alone together for an afternoon?"

"He's protecting my virtue. He likes me."

"He claims you are the only virgin west of the Rockies. I didn't think there were any at all in this city."

She always blushed when he spoke about it. Looking into the sea-blue eyes, she knew that she wanted Eric to be her lover, so it never made sense to her that she was quietly grateful for Phillip's persence.

"Let's go to your place," Eric said. She had never invited him there.

"I couldn't, really. It's not that kind of place."

"But Maija's not there afternoons and evenings."

"Just the same, I mean, her work is there and it's her place and well . . ."

"I told you. It's a convent."

"Secrets, secrets! What are you two whispering about, as if you think I can't hear through my cello. Eric, are you trying to seduce that girl again?"

Eric looked sullen. Again Elizabeth blushed. Phillip sat down on the arm of her chair, and she thought what a shame that he was so pudgy for a young man. But it didn't matter; it went with him, with his spontaneous laugh and the feeling he gave of watching her and quietly looking after her. It was he who had asked how old she was until she finally confessed to sixteen. "Aha," he had said wisely, as if it made a difference; then he had burst into a folksong, "I'll be sixteen next Sunday." He was playing with her, warning her, watching her and yet letting her know she was only an amusing kid who ought to be home.

"Come, Eric, you have to go play for your supper now. It's time."

"Damn, it goes so fast."

212

"And I really have to go too," Elizabeth said. "I'm only three-quarters of the way through that miserable test Maija is giving me."

Both Eric and Phillip were taking part in a string quartet that was doing a series of Sunday night performances at a coffee house. Eric had explained, "It's not just that I have to earn some money, but we're playing Haydn at the moment, and we're not sounding all that bad. Look, Liz, let's get together Sunday. We can borrow Phillip's car and go away somewhere and get back in time for the concert."

"Not on Sundays. I'm with Maija then."

"You sure have something going there," he said.

"Not what you think. . . . Well, I'm free, you know. I'll see."

It was true, she told herself on the way home; Maija made it clear that she was independent and there was no reason why Elizabeth shouldn't do the same. And yet, and yet . . .

Elizabeth was still thinking as she started up the stairs to the apartment. Nicholas bounced out to meet her, with a reproach; she didn't take him to the park anymore; she never came for dinner; she didn't play checkers with him.

She promised that she would, very soon, and as she unlocked her door, she realized that she was part of a family in a way — Maija, Sophie, Nicholas, Pete and Boris and even Dora Rainwater. She had not asked them to be concerned for her, yet in some slight way they were, just as in an unexpected way she had become concerned for them. Yet she was a free individual. And if she wanted to invite Eric over, why shouldn't she, she asked herself, surprised at the defiance in her voice.

# 43

Sunday took care of itself. Early in the morning, Maija woke Elizabeth up and said, "Come on, I've got a surprise downstairs."

Maija wouldn't say another word about it, but helped make a picnic lunch and dug out a jacket for Elizabeth to wear. Then she gave her a helmet and told her to put it on. She had one too that she had borrowed.

"A motorcycle?" Elizabeth asked fearfully. They frightened her.

"Isn't it great? I borrowed it for the day. We're going to go out and find the place for our Studio."

"Maija, you're crazy. You know how to drive one of those things?"

"My husband taught me. He wasn't all that useless, you see. Come on."

It was an appalling-looking beast-of-a-thing, Elizabeth said, and she was relieved when it wouldn't start. But Maija, swearing softly in Czechoslovakian, took out a tool kit, fussed here and there, and eventually got it started with a roar.

Elizabeth clung closely to Maija. If she were religious, she guessed, she would be muttering prayers until they got back again. She pressed close to Maija's strong back, shut her eyes as the cycle climbed, and shuddered as it rushed down the steep hills on the way out of the city.

Her first fears vanished as she realized Maija drove expertly, and she opened her eyes. They were flying! As they drove across the Golden Gate Bridge, she felt its sway, and her heart pumped with ecstasy as she looked up to the orange cathedral-high cable supports that thrust into the blue sky.

Maija turned off the main highway soon after leaving the bridge and headed for the steep narrow roads that twisted along the side of the mountains of Marin County. They passed through groves of pine and eucalyptus whose red and green scimitar-shaped leaves filtered the sunlight. Maija slowed down and stopped at a high grassy spot looking over a broad landscape of hills folding into other hills and beyond it all a glimpse of the Pacific.

"The silence is so sudden, you can hear it," Elizabeth said, as she removed her helmet and flopped down on the grass. She imagined Eric there, tickling her with a blade of grass, kissing her, and talking freely without Phillip or anyone else around. She was almost tempted to tell Maija about him, but instead found herself jumping into another matter.

"Tell me about David. Are you in love with him, Maija?"

Maija was gazing at a blackbird winging across the sky. "Next question. Is there something else you'd like to know?" Once this would have kept Elizabeth quiet, but not this time. Even though her better sense told her to be content with that answer, she went on.

"That's the question. About you and David. After all, I wouldn't want to be an interference."

"You *are* persistent! I will tell you some things and you can put the rest together yourself. His wife is a lovely dishwatery blonde, born well, is that how you say it? The whole society thing. And he is a moderately successful architect. More than that, he is public-spirited, particularly where art is concerned, and he likes to support it and so does she."

"That's it? You didn't answer the question."

"It's such a silly question."

She pressed herself against the earth, her head resting in her hands, looking off far into the distance. If it were not for men, how content they could both be. But here they were, both of them with their secrets, both of them waiting.

"Anyway," Maija said, "we're back on the road again and I'm hungry. I'll bet you are too. Besides, I'm looking for a place for The Studio. You see it around here anywhere?"

"Not really."

"Shall we go on, and then have lunch when we find it?" The way she spoke and the way she looked as she stood adjusting her helmet brought back their first trip together from Nebraska, and because it was now part of their history and so entire and precious in itself, Elizabeth found herself at ease with Maija once more. Confidently she placed herself on the seat behind Maija and pressed her head against the warm back, content.

"That's disgusting!" Maija blurted as the two houses on the other side of a hill turned out to be the first of a new tract, with the rounded landscape already laid out in lots. Riding on through the coastal area, they passed large houses half-hidden among carefully landscaped gardens and humble old farms that barely seemed to rise from the earth. After a few more miles the houses disappeared, the bare hills curved down to the ocean with occasional outcroppings of rock, and this time Maija stopped near a grove of wind-bent pines. In the distance a white house stood against a windbreak of cypress, and a herd of cows grazed in the pasture close by.

"That's it, Liz," Maija said. "The perfect place. The farmhouse could be the first headquarters, where we'd live and have our offices, a library, a guest house, or whatever. We'd have to build the rest. The studio itself, where we work, well, what do you think it should be like? I keep seeing it as a round building, perhaps with a row of small studios off at one side, like a panhandle. Eventually we'd build cabins, or rammed-earth houses, for living quarters; people have to be alone some of the time. And hens, we should keep hens, maybe a cow. Or goats. What do you think about goats?"

"I don't think about them very much, if you must know," Elizabeth said, amused. Surely Maija was the biggest daydreamer she had ever met, but she might as well play along. "I suppose we'd have a big organic garden. And, come to think of it, Katina could take care of the goats, long-haired goats of course. And maybe we could have a few camels so we could get camel-hair."

"Why not?" Maija said lightly, but Elizabeth wondered if perhaps she had hurt her feelings. "Let's have some lunch, shall we?"

"I was kidding about the camels, Maija, but I like the idea of the round studio. We'll have to have a fireplace, right? And it won't be just women there, will it?"

"Don't worry. There'll be a place for men. If they can

design and weave, that is. There's lots of pain with men, Liz, but . . . well, you have to take it as it comes. But The Studio will be a whole new way of life, don't you see, a way of working and of living, and I think that the man and woman thing will be the least of our worries. There'll be financing to think about at first . . ."

Elizabeth placed a sandwich in her hand and a cup of coffee, and said, like a tolerant mother listening to her child dreaming, "Let's have the sandwiches first and worry about the finances after, all right?"

Maija, catching the innuendo, grinned, but Elizabeth knew, as she stared at the farmhouse set in the hills, that Maija was already seeing The Studio and the gardens with the goats outside and the artists weaving and, for all she knew, even the tapestry on the loom. As for Elizabeth, she saw what was there, the brown and empty hills and the farmhouse that belonged to someone else.

# 44

The early afternoons were sweet and then grew sweeter because Eric was there but soon would be gone. Even now, their hours were limited because Eric had rehearsals with the quartet, a few pupils to teach, the stint as street musician which was so lucrative he couldn't afford to give it up, and night performances. But on that particular day they walked along the shops of Union Street, stopped at a café for coffee, and sat in the dark room with all the light glistening outside. He took her hand.

"I'm furious with Phillip. Pupils half the time, practicing the other half. And I want you so. I dream of you, Liz. Why don't we go to your place?"

"I want you too. I suppose it's time I 'grew up,' only, our place is . . . Well, for one thing it's uncomfortable. We sleep on these narrow beds."

"There's never been a bed too narrow for that."

"And the neighbors are nosy . . ."

"You worry about that, for Pete's sake? Well, anyway, I'd like to see the place; is that permitted? I want to see this tapestry you're always talking about. I'd like to meet Maija too."

"I guess I could show you what we're doing there. Maybe it is a good idea. Then you'll see what it's like for us."

"You are a darling, Liz, you really are. And such a handsome girl. Can we go now?"

"Just for a little while," she said hesitantly.

She hoped nobody would see them as they climbed the stairs to the apartment.

"So this is it! Good lord, that tapestry is enormous! And . . ." he whistled "I wish I could see it finished. It's impressive. And that's what you do too?"

"Me? Oh no, I'm just a beginner. Here's my loom. This is the problem piece. As you can tell, it's a problem."

"Not at all. I like it, Liz. I do."

"Want to see some more of Maija's work? I have a photograph album with pictures of her work; she's done so much and she's still so young."

"Some other time. Why don't you show me the apartment?"

"All right," she said showing him the kitchen, and the bathtub that stood on little claw feet. She opened the bedroom door for a second and shut it again, but he embraced her, kissed her, and opening the door drew her in. Immediately, she resisted, pulling away.

"Listen, I don't like this, Eric. You know that."

"Then why did you take me up here?"

"You wanted to see the tapestries."

He laughed a little as though she must be dense. "Yes, that's true, but mostly I wanted to see *you*."

She laughed uncomfortably. He sounded false. What had seemed so reasonable and desirable when they were on a street corner or in a restaurant now became tawdry in that small bedroom with its two narrow beds.

"I'm sorry, Eric, it's something I can't do, not here. I didn't even know I'd feel that way."

"Christ," he said, taking out a cigarette and lighting it, while Elizabeth picked up Lotus and held her close, as though Lotus would protect her. This seemed to infuriate Eric even more. He sat down on Maija's stool and squinted at Elizabeth through the smoke.

"Do you know what I think? I think that you and Maija just don't need any men around."

"Oh no, Eric, that's a terrible thing to imply. I'm not what you think . . ."

"Why can't you say the words the way they are? I've never seen such a Victorian. Say 'dyke' if you mean it, don't hedge around like that."

"I'll speak the way I want, Eric. I am straight and so is Maija; in fact, there's no question about it. It's just . . . oh Eric, don't think I'm frigid or frightened.

It's just that this is Maija's place, can't you understand, and it's not a place where I can do that."

"And you would somewhere else? You're sure it's just the place?"

"I think so." She didn't know what she thought; what if she were frigid, unable to love? A new fear.

"I'll be leaving in eight days, Liz. Would you come with me?"

"To L.A.? Do you mean it?"

"Sure. Then we can both be free, you of Maija and me of Phillip. Not that they're not wonderful people and all that, but there's a time when changes have to be made. And, I didn't tell you this, I'm not sure about it, but it's likely I'll be house-sitting for someone in Bel Air, a small and absolutely perfect little house with a pool. After this place — good lord, how do you stand it without rugs? — that will be heaven. And you'll get to know lots of real people, people who've made it, and I'll let you sleep late in the mornings."

Her eyes were shining. "It would be nice to be comfortable, and if Maija weren't there, I know we wouldn't have any trouble, and well, it is kind of exciting to think about, isn't it?"

"You'll go?"

"It will be awfully hard to tell Maija."

"She'll understand. Anyway, I won't push you today, my lovely, but it's a disappointment. Come with me and we'll make up for it."

Her face was burning and she felt dizzy, as though she had had too much wine.

"It's just that I can't believe it yet. But I'll go, Eric, I'll go."

# 45

The following Tuesday morning was the day Elizabeth would leave with Eric, and it was agreed that she would be waiting with her bags packed. She told herself little stories and made promises all week, "You will go swimming every day, you will go to the concerts under the stars, you will find new clothes, you will go to some parties for a change, somebody will see you, somebody from the movies and say what a beautiful girl you are, and come down and we'll give you a screen test."

She had to tell herself these stories because every time she looked over and saw Maija patiently and deftly weaving the yarns in and out, she felt a flush of guilt. She worked furiously on the tapestry that tired her so, and Maija was pleased that she wanted it to be finished so soon.

On the weekend she scrubbed the apartment. On Sunday when Maija asked if she would mind working for the morning because she didn't want to fall behind the deadline, Elizabeth agreed. And in the afternoon when Maija wanted to go to the island that was in the middle of Stowe Lake at Golden Gate Park, she agreed without a murmur.

"I don't know why I want to go there so much," Maija said. "It's a place I like very much. Well, why not?"

So they had walked around the island and sat and watched the lovers and families and kids in the boats in the lake below. And still Elizabeth didn't tell her.

That night she phoned Eric. "Can't you possibly call for me in the afternoon on Tuesday? It would be easier for me." She was thinking that she wouldn't tell Maija at all but would leave her a note.

"N.O. No. It will take us seven or eight hours to get down to L.A. And I have commitments. You understand."

"Oh sure. Well, I guess I'll be ready."

On Monday night her bags were packed and ready under the bed. On Tuesday morning she sat nervously, working on her tapestry, when the bell rang below. She could hear his steps, and then he was knocking at the door.

"Who's that?" Maija asked. Elizabeth drew herself in and seemed to freeze, so Maija went to the door.

"Hello, I guess you're Maija? We meet at last. I'm Eric. How are you?" He held out his hand, stood there confident and cheerful, almost too handsome, Elizabeth thought.

"I saw your work and I want you to know I think you are superb!" Elizabeth felt she was shrinking fast and had she been able to disappear, she would have done so. "Hey, Liz are you ready?"

"Just a minute. Who are you and what is Liz supposed to be ready for?" Maija demanded.

"You mean she didn't tell you? Liz, what's the matter with you?" he said, while Elizabeth's face turned scarlet and for a tense moment she thought she was going to be sick.

"Will you please come in and shut the door and then

tell me what this is all about. Liz, do you know this man?"

She nodded. But she seemed unable to talk.

"Maybe I'd better explain," Eric said. "You know, don't you, that Elizabeth and I have been seeing each other almost every day."

Maija's face blanched white. "No, I didn't know that at all."

"Good God, Liz, did you expect to keep it a secret? It's like this, Maija. We're in love, in a way, that is. I'm going to L.A. to try out for a chair in the symphony there with a reasonable chance of getting it, and Liz has decided to move in with me. I'm sorry she didn't tell you. Come on, Liz, it's getting late and we have a long trip."

"Just a minute," Maija said. "I thought at first you might have been her brother. You look somewhat alike, you know. This is the first I've heard about you or about Liz's leaving. Let me gather myself together for a moment, will you?"

She walked over to the window, looked out, then turned around with her arms folded and her head shaking almost imperceptibly. "If this is what you want, Liz, all right. It's terribly sudden. But I have no hold on you. You're free."

Elizabeth trembled as if she were freezing, looked up at Maija, and then turned to Eric. When she spoke, her voice was scarcely audible. "I've changed my mind, Eric. I'm not going. I intended to go, but you see, well, I haven't finished my tapestry yet." She smiled vaguely with this lame excuse, as though imploring him not to be too angry.

"Come off it, Liz. You know you want to go. You've

224

been talking about it all week long. I know you want to go. You need a change. You've just got the jitters."

"No. No, Eric. I'm really sorry. It must seem as if I misled you on purpose, but I didn't mean to. I just can't leave."

"Why the hell can't you?"

"Because I can't. I can't think of reasons. It's just that it isn't right and it isn't going to work. I didn't even think this out, but I felt it a little. And now I know it's true. It just wouldn't work."

Eric put his hands on his hips. His face was red with anger. He stamped forward until he stood in front of her, and Maija moved closed to Elizabeth, afraid he might attack her.

"You are a crazy female. Do you hear that? You are a crazy female and you're going to get crazier if you stay around here! It's clear now that I see Maija. Don't think I can't tell about you girls who want to be together."

"Just a minute," Maija broke in sternly. "Watch what you say. You're all wrong. You have no right to say that."

"I have a right to say I don't know what your game is, Elizabeth, but it's your life, isn't it? And maybe it's just as well that I found out now, before it's too late. I know what you are."

"Please, Eric. It's not what you think. And I did think a lot of you and I wish you good luck and I'm sorry for all the trouble, but it would be the wrong thing to do . . ."

He laughed bitterly. "Baby, you are beautiful but you are all screwed up!"

With that he turned and left, slamming the door. The

225

girls stood frozen as they heard him going down the stairs. Elizabeth put her hands over her face and began to shake. First came the crying, in gasping sobs, then the laughing that tore from her until she stood there hysterical and on the verge of screaming. She felt that she was running toward a cliff and would jump off before she could stop, and the laughing and sobbing came all the harder until something sharp struck her face, first one side, then the other. And the craziness stopped. And there was Maija, not slapping her anymore but standing there. Elizabeth fell to the floor sobbing.

Maija sat on the floor beside her and waited. At last Elizabeth lifted red bleary eyes. "I'm so ashamed," she said. "How can you ever forgive me?"

"I don't know," Maija said, her face still pale and the dark eyes sad as though they had seen so much pain already. "But you're still here. I'm still here. Do you want to stay?"

She nodded soberly. The girls sat together on the floor for a long time. Then Maija made tea and the hot liquid warmed them.

"I'm going to call and say I won't be in to work today," Maija said. "And then, I think we both ought to take a walk, maybe by the ocean."

The day seemed to have no time. Once they stopped by the sea wall and Maija asked, "Did you really love him?"

"I thought maybe I did. It was a mistake. I make so many mistakes. I run away every time something gets hard. No character, no faith."

"You didn't run this time," Maija said. "I would have let you go, if you'd wanted."

She nodded and put her hand on Maija's. Then for no reason they could think of, they sighed because the danger was past, and then they laughed because they felt something very much like happiness in being together.

# 46

"Now that it's over, I'm so happy, Maija. I can hardly *believe* it. If only it would last . . ."

"The first mistake is to look for permanence. Change, big change or little change, that's the way it goes. So when your good days come . . ."

"Love them like flowers, right?" Elizabeth answered. She had finished the test tapestry and was now busy sewing the slits together and finishing off the edges.

"I'm afraid I still don't like this much. It was a problem and it still looks like that to me."

"Keep it anyway. It's a kind of vocabulary of skills. Compare it with your first one and you'll see how far you've come along. Once that's finished, we'll begin some other techniques. Phew, it's hot, isn't it!"

The foggy coolness of August which was proper for a San Francisco summer had given way to an unprecedented heat wave.

"And I thought the Central Valley was bad!" Elizabeth said, drops of perspiration on her forehead and upper lip. These steaming days she wore a striped sleeveless jersey, and her hair was pulled to the top of her head in a loose knot from which a blond strand escaped here and there.

The windows were open and the sounds of the city seemed harsher and angrier than ever, the shrieking of brakes, the labored roar of fire engines and always the sirens, ambulance, fire and police.

"People can't take too much heat," Maija said. "The crime rate has almost doubled in the last week, as if it weren't bad enough already."

However, the temperature didn't keep the girls from working. Since that emotional Tuesday when Eric had left, the tension between the girls had relaxed and Maija worked furiously fast on *The Phoenix* so that she would have time to show Elizabeth the non-loom techniques, knotting, braiding, wrapping, finger weaving.

"What you have to remember," she said," is that they are only techniques, and technique alone is never enough. You have to have something to say, and all of this is only a means of saying it. Otherwise, you'll turn out meaningless diddily wall hangings that look like a million other diddily hangings made by bored housewives. You understand?"

Elizabeth knew. She was already aware of what was a cliché and how few genuine statements there were. Her mind was beginning to teem with fragments of ideas and her fingers were growing supple and clever.

She remembered the story Maija had once told her about how she had touched the vertical threads in the weaving room that first time and how the threads seemed to stream between her fingers and heaven. The priest had understood; it was a religious experience.

"I know it won't happen to me the same way," she told Maija, "but there must be some sign, some confirmation that weaving is right for me too."

228

"You can't will an experience or a confirmation and you can't hurry it. You have to wait, work and wait. If you think about it too much, it will fly away, like the *Bird of Happiness*. So you might as well let it happen. After all, what else can you do?"

Elizabeth looked at Maija's uplifted profile as she concentrated on inserting lengths of flax into *The Phoenix'* wings, and the fear left. Maija said the understanding would come and she, Elizabeth, believed it. Lotus jumped up on her lap and played with a strand of her hair that had come loose. The sun poured in the window bathing everything in a richness of golden light with fiery edges and deep shadows.

She had never felt closer to happiness.

Three days later on a Saturday when she expected Maija home at six-thirty, she polished the kitchen to a gleaming finish and decided to celebrate with a special sort of dinner. Celebrate what, Maija would ask. Just us, she would reply. Isn't that enough?

Remembering the special summer meals her mother always carried off so well, she made a design of cold marinated vegetables in radiating circles on a large round plate, the sharp reds of the tomatoes and radishes challenging the light and dark greens in perfect harmony. The can of tuna and black olives made it a salade Niçoise. A bowl of fruits to follow. Candles on the table. A centerpiece of the diaphanous gold and white outer peels of onions held together to suggest flowers. The tiny rolls Maija loved.

Six-thirty passed, then seven, and Maija didn't come home. Elizabeth, meeting Sophie in the hall, asked her if she'd seen her, but Sophie shook her head. She stopped downstairs, thinking that perhaps Boris had invited her in for a glass of wine, as he sometimes did, but he hadn't seen her either.

An uneasiness filled the apartment but she didn't permit herself to panic. Not knowing what to do, she finally decided to walk toward the Launderette in hopes of meeting her along the way. As she walked down Post Street she realized that Maija might have taken another way home, or quite possibly David had called for her. Elizabeth threaded her way through the tourists and locals dressed up for a Saturday night on the town, but Maija wasn't among them. She crossed the street and immediately the Saturday night gaiety changed to a cheerless emptiness.

As she passed the drugstore on the corner, she was aware of men watching her and one of them called, "Hey, chick, you back again?" They whispered jokes and burst into laughter of which she was without doubt the butt. Never mind them, she told herself; she had to find Maija. The coming darkness didn't make it easier.

She knew that Maija usually left the lights burning before she went home, so Elizabeth was disturbed to find the Launderette unlit and the door unlocked. She went inside, now afraid, since it was too dark to see anything.

"Maija?" she called out uncertainly, and when there was no answer, fear sent shivers along her spine.

There had to be a light switch somewhere. She fumbled by the door, found it, flicked it on and stood there while a weak overhead light lit up the silent rows of washing machines and dryers and the eight empty wooden chairs in the middle of the room. She swallowed as her throat became dry. A panic she could not stop paralyzed her; she stood rooted to the spot.

230

In the dim light she saw a long white thing extending from behind the stand where the cash register stood. She took a step closer and saw that it was Maija's outstretched arm as she lay unconscious on the floor.

She screamed, but the scream made no sound. She ran over and bent down beside Maija to see if she was still alive, putting her ear to her heart. "Thank God," she said; its beat was slow but it was beating still. Maija's breathing was shallow and her face already had a waxy distant pallor.

"Maija! Maija!" she called in anguish.

Now a calm voice within told her exactly what to do. There was no telephone at the Launderette, but she remembered seeing one in a booth at a gas station in the next block. She ran to it and called the police. They told her to wait with Maija and they would come and send an ambulance.

So there was nothing to do but wait. She knelt by Maija and prayed, something she had almost never done in her life. As she felt Maija's coldness, she looked around for a blanket and found a baby quilt in a basket of clean wash. If only she knew what else to do . . . She knelt by Maija, rubbed her cold hands, talked to her, coaxed her to open her eyes, and assured her it was only a bad dream from which they would both wake up.

How long it took the police and ambulance to come, she could not tell. When they arrived, they immediately began asking questions, while the ambulance men placed Maija on a stretcher, folding her arms as though she were already dead. It was quickly concluded that Maija had been attacked with a blunt instrument and the register had been robbed. One of them yawned as he spoke, but at least he said Elizabeth could go to the hospital with Maija. She stepped in the ambulance, and the men closed the door behind her.

"It's a nightmare. I'll wake up soon," she comforted herself, shivering in the hot, close night.

While she waited for Maija to be X-rayed, Elizabeth called David Kazarian. The phone rang four times before he answered. He apologized for being so slow; he had been on his way out. Elizabeth blurted out what had happened and she could feel him being thrown into shock, as though the rigidity of it passed through the telephone wires. After a silence he asked in a low restrained voice where Maija was and said he would be right over.

"Is there a chance for her?" he asked Elizabeth later in the hospital room, his face as pallid as hers, his evening clothes incongruous.

"Maybe. The doctors refuse to say. She's been hit hard and it's a bad fracture."

"Oh no," he groaned. He sank into the stiff chair by the bed and sat there, head in hands, his eyes never leaving Maija's still form. Each labored breath was a miracle.

"How could this happen to Maija, of all people! Maija! Oh my God."

His voice broke with grief. Elizabeth would not have been surprised if he had yelled violently, so deep was his anger. But his shock and grief turned to silence. The two of them sat there numb.

A nurse offered to bring them coffee. No, thanks. She urged Elizabeth to go out for something to eat, to go home and sleep and come back the next day, because Maija's condition would be unlikely to change for at least ten hours, perhaps more. David urged her to do as the nurse suggested but she shook her head. He said he had to leave but would be in touch.

After midnight, Elizabeth fell asleep and someone put her on a cot in a room next door. When she woke up two hours later, she was furious with herself for having left Maija for even one minute.

Time had no meaning. There was nothing to do but wait. As dawn began to come, Maija's eyes opened slowly and found Elizabeth who was bending over her.

"Maija!"

Maija recognized her with an almost imperceptible nod. She almost managed the beginning of a smile, but the lips froze and her eyes began to glaze.

The nurse explained that she was in a coma and the doctor would be there soon, although there was little anyone could do. She urged Elizabeth to sleep but she refused.

"I'll be back in a little while," the nurse said in a voice so hushed that Elizabeth knew she had no hope for Maija's life.

Elizabeth refused to give up. She held the chilled hands and in quivering words begged Maija to come back. When the doctor came, he took her hand away and told Elizabeth that Maija was dead.

# 47

The fog had drifted back to the city that morning, a mist of grief, but the chill Elizabeth suffered had nothing to do with the weather. When David came, all she

could say was, "I'm so cold, you know. I'm freezing."
He had held her and they grieved together in that
first shocked silence.

He took her to his home, and his wife, the dishwater
blonde who really seemed to have no color whatever,
insisted on making tea for Elizabeth and pouring a
hot bath for her. She took her to the guest room and
though it was warm enough and the satin sheets and
brown quilt were soothing, she shivered for a long
time before falling into a deep, black sleep.

Later David came to talk with her. They must make
the funeral arrangements, for he didn't think she had
any relatives on the coast. Would a cremation be proper,
did she think? Were there friends who might want to
attend? She was not to worry; he would take care of
the details.

Time passed irrationally like a nightmare, both slowly
and quickly. Later she remembered sitting in a small
chapel with a few of Maija's friends, Sophie, Katina,
Boris and Nicholas and other people she had never
seen before, waiting in a strange silence for the service
to begin. Someone played a Bach solo on the flute, its
lone clear sound filling the chapel. David spoke and
she listened to the sound of his voice, but she didn't
hear what he said. Then they waited while the coffin
slid into the opening and was consumed in flames.

Katina invited Elizabeth home, and David thought
it would be best if she spent the next few days at their
house, but she felt she must go back to the apartment.
Shuddering, she opened the door.

*The Phoenix* was still there, its brilliant colors burning in the gray afternoon. She walked to the kitchen
and found the table still set for the two of them, the

fragile onion flowers papery and still. The heavy blue sweater Maija sometimes wore hung on a hook near the back door, and an open book which she had been reading before going to work lay on the bed.

Emptiness.

She sat at the stool in front of *The Phoenix*, picked up a bobbin, and idly wrapped yarn around it as though she were about to use it, but she only sat there, dry-eyed and wan.

The knock on the door was so soft she didn't hear it until it was repeated more loudly. The third time, she walked heavily and opened the door to find Dora standing there, holding out to her a plastic pot with a cypress seedling six inches high, a straight dark green line.

"Here," Dora said, putting it in Elizabeth's hands. "For Maija."

For the first time since she had known her, Dora looked directly at Elizabeth. She understands this, Elizabeth knew at that moment; Dora could understand pain, death, and utter helplessness.

"Thank you. Maija would be pleased. It is a beautiful thing to do."

Dora turned and shuffled down the stairs, and Elizabeth put the pot on the floor beside the loom. The twenty-nine-cent price tag was still glued on.

She sat on Maija's stool and the tears began to come. She wept and wept until she could weep no more. Then she stumbled into bed and slept until noon the next day.

# 48

In the confusion of waking, she thought she heard Maija in the kitchen putting on the coffee. She jumped out of bed and ran to the kitchen, but it was empty, the table still set for the celebration dinner.

She wandered aimlessly through the apartment. A familiar mew at the door brought her to life and she let Lotus in. She picked her up and held her close, offered her milk, but she wasn't hungry. Someone, perhaps Boris, had watched out for Lotus in the days since Maija's death.

Elizabeth felt the emptiness of the apartment oppressive, suggesting to her what the world would be like if everyone had gone. And yet, there was *The Phoenix* in the middle of the room. And unfinished though he was, he seemed to be alive. He stood there with his dignified head — not quite complete — raised high as he looked around him, while below flames curled upward, spiralling into leaves. As many times as she had seen it, living with it day after day, she seemed to be understanding it now for the first time.

"What will happen to him? What a pity he's not finished," she said, touching the wing that was completed.

*The Phoenix* was a little more than two-thirds done. The legs, outstretched wings, much of the body and some of the tail were worked in brilliant reds, blues and purples. The rest of the outline was visible in meticulous ink-made points that surrounded each warp, indicating the change in color and pattern. What would happen to it? She supposed David could hire someone to finish it, but the thought of a stranger touching Maija's work filled her with anger. Again the senselessness of the crime overwhelmed her so that she could not think for awhile.

"Nobody else could do it," she said to herself out loud. How would they know where to keep the work thin and where to build it out thick, where to raise it like a bas-relief and where to wind the yarns? One day, she remembered, Maija had called her over to show her how to give the effect of a thin yarn floating over the surface, to suggest a quivering current of air, something Maija herself had devised. Nobody else would even know this.

Elizabeth picked up the bobbin almost without thinking. The leaf would not be too difficult to finish and she might as well do it. Next to it lay the creamy white background and certainly she knew she could manage that. If it didn't work out, she promised an invisible Maija, she would rip it out and do it over.

One thing led to another. She worked for an hour, then stepped back to see if she could tell where Maija's work ended and hers began, or if there was any difference in the tension. It seemed consistent.

She stood back even further, still in her nightgown, her bare feet getting cold on the wooden floor. She breathed a deep satisfying breath and the chill seemed to relax.

"Maija would want me to finish it," she said, knowing this had to be right.

Then she ran to get washed, dressed, and have breakfast, for she was suddenly starving. Afterward she would get back to work.

# 49

Late that afternoon David Kazarian came, a bouquet of marguerites in one hand and a package wrapped in butcher paper in the other.

"Hello, Elizabeth. How are you?"

"All right. And you? Please come in."

"This is for you," he said offering her the flowers, "and you can probably use this too. I always wondered how you managed on Maija's near macrobiotic diet. You probably need a steak at this point."

"How nice! Won't you share the steak with me?"

"Sorry, my wife will be expecting me."

"Well, can I make you some tea?"

"That would be very nice. I suppose we have things to settle."

He followed Elizabeth to the kitchen, and while she put on the water for tea and arranged the flowers in a vase, he studied the postcards and photographs Maija had pinned to the wall. Snapshots of Maija standing at a huge loom, Maija at a tapestry show, Maija standing with several people he guessed were her family. David studied these for a long time, and when he turned to Elizabeth, she thought his face showed the strain and grief she understood so well.

238

"Were you in love with her?" Elizabeth asked.

"Of course. You did know that, didn't you? Only there was no answer to it, you know. My marriage, other commitments . . . Yes, I loved her very much. And admired her." His voice broke off but he recovered, becoming his suave self once more. "And you, has it been a bad day for you?"

"I don't dare to think of it that way. I'm still frozen at the core, a little. Can we talk about *The Phoenix*? What did you plan to do about it?"

"Good lord, that's one problem I hadn't come to yet. Of course. Well, I don't know."

"Come with me, won't you?" She led him to the other room. "Can you tell where my work begins? I've done a little on it."

"You're that advanced, Liz? No, I can't tell. Do you think you could finish it? It would be the most logical thing for you to do, wouldn't it?"

"I'd like to think so. It's presumptuous, of course. But I'd like to try. I have the cartoon so I can do it pretty much as she wanted, and we could always rip it out if it didn't work."

He took her hand. "Do you think you can get it done in, let's see, two and a half weeks?"

"Perhaps. I can try."

"Bless you, Liz. Maija herself would be most pleased. As for the practical things, order whatever yarns you need, and there'll be enough money coming in on it to pay you. We can figure it out later. I can help you now if you're short."

"Thanks. I'm glad to be able to do it. I'm not worried about the money or anything. Not now."

They went back to the kitchen, and David sat where

Maija had always had her chair. The light of the city faded while they sipped more tea and he became a dark profile against the window.

"I'm worried about your living alone," he said.

"Please don't. I would have been frightened about it at one time, but Maija's taught me how to live with myself." Tears threatened for a moment but she blinked them back. "Sophie next door is good to me, and there's Katina if I'm desperate, and Boris and Nicholas are friendly. Only, I don't really feel alone. It's as if Maija were here with me, with us."

"It's been said that people do not die right away but hover around for awhile. So maybe Maija is still looking after you."

He put his large hand over hers, and silently they watched the twilight darken the purple sky. He asked after a while, "What shall we do with her ashes? Scatter them at sea?"

"I think she would like that."

"There are practical matters too. Will you go through her belongings and find out who her relatives and friends are so we can inform them? And one more thing: I think I'll collect as much of her work as I can and buy it up or see that it gets into museums that will be glad to have it and show it. Perhaps you can help me?"

"I'll do all I can."

"I know. If you need anything at all, Liz, or if you are lonely, will you call me? I feel somewhat responsible for you now."

"Thanks. I'll be all right."

They sat together and there was no more to say, The marguerites glowed white and the teacups sat on the table, their edges shining in the fading light. A calm sadness hovered in the air.

"This is our memoriam for Maija. This, right now," she said.

He nodded. After a few minutes, he kissed her gently and left.

# 50

"I gotta have more green and orange and lots of red, 'Lizabeth, 'cause this is a magic turtle and I'm gonna tie him to the chair," Nicholas said. He was sitting on the floor creating his own tapestries on the rungs of a kitchen chair while Elizabeth sat at *The Phoenix*.

"And then I'm gonna tie him to the doorknob so he'll bite anyone who comes in," he continued. "Hell, Liz, I'm all knotted up. Come help me."

"Don't say 'Hell,' Nicholas, it isn't nice," Elizabeth said softly as she slipped off her stool, knelt by Nicholas, and helped untangle his turtle.

"And then I'm gonna make a cave and we'll keep him in a cave," he said.

"Nicholas, you're going to knot up the whole room and we'll have to stay here forever," she said. He laughed. More than once Boris had left the little boy with her while he ran errands. He was something of a nuisance, that was true, but in some way he was healing the deep wound of Maija's death.

*The Phoenix* was almost complete. For three weeks

now she had picked up the bobbins and worked from one end of the loom to the other and now the proud head of *The Phoenix*, completed at last, looked out as if to say, so this is the world! Some of the areas had been troublesome, and she had done them over two or three times. Nor was the cartoon as completely drawn as she would have liked, so she had to make decisions about certain areas. At times she wondered if she would finish it soon enough. But David was pleased with her progress.

"Necessity is a good teacher," he said, sounding like Maija, sounding like her father too.

The door opened slowly and Nicholas cried, "Oh Boris, wait! I just got my turtle all tied up! He'll bite you but he won't bite Liz or me."

"So I'm the odd man out. Will your turtle not bite me if I invite Elizabeth to have dinner with us tonight?"

Nicholas danced around to show him the weaving he had done earlier that afternoon with strips of paper, and Boris thanked Elizabeth. She promised to have dinner with them if they would forgive her for leaving right after. She had a tight schedule.

"Of course. Six o'clock? Let's do something, a fabulous creation from Julia C., what do you say, Nicholas?"

"I love them," Elizabeth thought as they left. She wondered at the fact that recently she found herself using the word "love" so frequently.

She turned to *The Phoenix*, running her hands over him lightly once more. The creamy white of the handspun background was warm and soft, as though it contained within it the spring of life itself. Passing the fibers in and out of the warp, she could almost feel it breathing and herself breathing along with it.

She was part of it now, or it was part of her. They were one and the same. That confirmation, that nod that said yes, this is for you, had come, through her fingers, through her own breath, and she knew it as surely as she could know anything.

If only Maija knew! But perhaps she was there, perhaps she did know.

Boris's rich baritone called from below to tell her dinner was ready. As she washed and ran the brush through her hair, she looked at *The Phoenix* again, almost as though she were seeing it for the first time. It was rising from its flames to begin a new life.

"I'm *The Phoenix*," she said. And it seemed so simple and so exactly right that she found herself wondering and then laughing.

Boris called again and she skipped freely down the stairs.

# 51

At last it was finished. She cut it, freeing it from the loom, sewed together what splits she thought Maija would want joined, and was even humming the song Maija used to hum when Sophie walked in with a plate of cheese buns.

"It's done! A miracle. That Maija was a strange girl, but an angel, a good person like you seldom see. You know how I could tell? My dogs loved her like they love you. My dogs don't make mistakes."

"I like them too," Elizabeth said, "and if I have one, I'll bring him to you to be groomed."

"Thank you," Sophie said seriously, "and for every customer you bring, ten percent off. So what are you going to do now the tapestry is finished? Where will you go? You can't live alone. Anyway, how could you afford it? You want to move in with me? I have a room. I always wanted a daughter like you. And I won't charge."

Again Elizabeth thanked her. Everyone was so kind. The sound of two dogs barking on the stairway and a cat hissing somewhere below saved Elizabeth from having to answer, as Sophie rushed out to greet another customer.

The next day David came, admired the tapestry, and rolled it up so that he could take it to the professionals who would arrange for the final mounting. Once it was gone, the apartment seemed empty as though its spirit had fled.

Elizabeth lay on her bed not quite believing *The Phoenix* was gone. How often when she had worked on it had she thought she would never finish. Now that it was gone, she knew she must gather her possessions and leave too.

Maija was the artist and she was only the assistant. What belonged to her then? A few small tapestries and a book of sketches. She was humble, for *The Phoenix* had shown her she was still a beginner.

Her eyes rested on the *Maru* tapestry. She had seen it so often she had begun to take it for granted. Now she saw it with fresh eyes. For the first time, she knew what it could mean.

"If it could all be put into one word," Maija had said, "the love, the devotion, the caring . . ."

244

Elizabeth decided to ask one favor of David Kazarian, to let her keep that tapestry. It was hers now by right and by understanding. *Maru* belonged to her.

Sophie's question hung in the air. Where would she go next?

The next day she walked, deciding to visit all the places she had been to with Maija. She had coffee and cheese buns at the Russian restaurant on Clement Street, stopped in at the shops and museums and galleries where they sometimes lingered, returned library books, wandered through Golden Gate Park. She walked through the marble halls of the De Young Museum, pretending that Maija was with her, but when she saw her reflection in a glass, she knew she was alone. There are many funeral marches, not just one.

From there she walked along the road, stopping to admire the tree ferns because Maija had liked them. She rested in the hidden bit of meadow where they used to go to sun themselves. At Stowe Lake, like an unchanging movie set, children were still feeding the ducks, old people were strolling with their dogs, and rowboats glided easily across the lake.

What to do now?

Get a job? But what could she do? Wait on tables, become a clerk, go on relief?

That wasn't it at all.

"Maija," she spoke to the wind, "you know. I want to be a weaver, like you. But where do I go now? What do I do?"

She crossed to the island in the middle of the lake, the place Maija had loved so much. The pine tree sang the answer. Go home.

To her mother? Her father? But her mother couldn't

manage with her there. Her father could, but what about Lorene? For the first time in months she thought about her and realized she no longer hated her. "Why, that poor woman, she's doing what she can, the best she can."

And although it might be hard for Elizabeth to like her very much, her father did need Lorene. Maybe, if Elizabeth weren't so nasty, Lorene would seem different. She must need people too.

Need. That was the word. Throughout the long walk home, the word kept coming back. She had needed Maija. Her father needed Lorene. But he needed his daughter too. So did Mark. And she could do so much for Patty, sweet Patty! How long it was since she'd even thought about her.

If she went home, perhaps she could study weaving at the University while she was still in high school. Then she wouldn't have to be home so much.

The wind was blowing cold and it seemed about to rain. She passed richly dressed women with well-manicured poodles, young couples talking intimately as they passed her, a small Japanese woman herding what must have been a class of youngsters, like a mother quail guiding her chattering young across the road. A young bearded man looked at Elizabeth as if he would like to stop and talk.

She loved the city. Every bit of it. Some day she would make her home here. But now, without Maija, it was empty.

Too tired to make up her mind, confused with wanting to stay and wanting to leave, she walked up the stairs to her room, pausing outside Boris's apartment. Pete must have been home, for the hi-fi was louder than usual, and the sweet familiar sounds of the Mozart quintet floated through the dark hall. The poignant phrases were threads leading her to her father. How much she suddenly wanted to see him again!

So it was Mozart who solved her problem. She bustled downstairs, and after stopping to get change from Mr. Hommada, stepped into the telephone booth on the corner, dropped a coin, and waited until the operator asked her what she wanted.

"If you please, I'd like to make a collect call to Lincoln, Nebraska."

# 52

Three days later Elizabeth stood in the San Francisco airport, waiting to board the plane. The jets, moving close to the observation window, became gigantic birds or fish. Totems of the day.

Her friends stood in a small circle waiting with her. David and Barbara Kazarian; Sophie, who insisted on giving her a loaf of homemade bread to bring to her father; Boris, Pete and Nicholas, who clung to her and didn't want her to go.

"I hardly recognize you without jeans and a jersey," Pete said. "Here you are looking like the society page."

Elizabeth laughed nervously. David had insisted on her taking the check for *The Phoenix*, and she had made one last trip to Magnin's, meeting her mother there. In a grand splash she had bought a shirt for her father, perfume for Lorene, something for the children, and for herself the soft gray dress and new shoes.

"And you looked perfectly lovely at the presentation of *The Phoenix* yesterday. Your mother was very proud. I'm glad she could come," Barbara said.

"You'll have to come back," David said. "You know, we'll need someone to make The Studio come to life."

"That was just a daydream, wasn't it? A nice one, but still a dream," Elizabeth said. If she had her way, she and David would talk for hours, as they already had, about Maija.

"It's not a daydream at all. That is, it's quite possible, Liz. Some people are interested, you know. You're going to go on with school, aren't you?"

"Yes, I expect to. Here. And in Europe, in the places where Maija studied."

"Then, you'll have to come back here someday."

"I will, David. I don't want to belong anywhere else."

The loudspeaker announced that passengers could board.

There was a sudden kissing and embracing, tears, and all the trite sayings that happen to be closest to the truth.

"Don't forget us."

"Come back, Liz. Remember, you can always stay with us."

"Come back *tomorrow*, 'Lizabeth!"

"Now, Nicholas. Elizabeth, you have given us so many happy evenings."

But it was David who took her hand and looked into her eyes. "You won't take Maija's place. Nobody can do that. But you'll have a place of your own. I'm sure of it."

248

"You . . . everyone . . . has been so wonderful."

The voice on the loudspeaker urged the passengers once more to get aboard.

"And if you don't hurry, you'll be visiting us tonight in San Francisco," David said, as he kissed her goodbye.

Elizabeth's friends moved to the observation window, and they thought they saw her wave through the window as the jet moved slowly across the field. It stopped, poised, for one minute at the end of the field. Then the vibrations sang through the air, and there was the suggestion of flame below as the great silver bird rose in the air and disappeared in the distance.